FURY OF
FRUSTRATION

COREENE
CALLAHAN

OLIVERHEBERBOOKS

1

THE OUTSKIRTS, ABERDEEN — SCOTLAND

He should've torched the place months ago. Struck a match and watched the fucker burn the second he finished reconning the area. The second he realized The White Hare wasn't an ordinary human waystation. The second the Parkland spoke to him and innkeeper derailed his plans.

Laying waste to the historic hotel, scaring the hell out of Mavis O'Donnell and the menagerie of strays she rolled out the red carpet for on a regular basis, would've served him better than what he'd done. Or rather...

What he'd *hadn't* done, then allowed to happen.

Contrails streaming off the tips of his horns, Kruger angled his wings into the wind. The dark webbing rippled as crisp air bit. His emerald-green, red-tipped scales shuddered in the blowback. Moonlight winked off his spiked spine. He tightened the cloaking spell, disappearing deeper into the web of invisibility, then blasted out of a tight turn.

Damp air slashed over interlocking dragon skin.

A slight adjustment, and his velocity downgraded from scale-splitting to smooth glide. The scent and sound of a clear spring night caught up with him. A hint of heather in the air. The call of one wolf to another. An exhilarating sense of something sharp rising on the west wind. Could be hope. Might be renewal. But more likely? The taste of victory as of yet unearned, but—

He growled in anticipation.

It wouldn't be long now. Tonight, in fact, if the next hour went his way. And honestly? After weeks of frustration, he needed it to go his way.

Gaze on the ground, he rocketed over thick forest and sliced over the ruins hidden in the underbrush. Treetops trembled. An unkindness of ravens cawed, nattering at him for disturbing the peace as he surveyed the Parkland. One hundred and seventy-three hectares of beauty comprising old-growth trees, winding streams, and rumbling waterfalls. None of it his, though that would change soon.

The innkeeper had no choice but to agree to his terms now. She was done. Finished. Cornered, with no friends left to call on. He'd changed tactics *again*, sealing her fate, ensuring his victory even if Mavis didn't know it yet.

Turning north, he flew over a winding river. Water rushed over rock, playing in the hallows, rumbling three hundred feet below him. Mist wicking from his scales, he followed the twists and turns, then made for the main road. Single lane. Unpaved. Squat stone walls galloping along each side. The only way in or out of the Parkland, at least by car.

Thick woodland smoothed into rolling fields, then opened onto manicured lawns and gardens beyond the front gate. Hundred-year-old oaks lined the main drive, canopies curving inward, leafy heads bowed in welcome. At the top of the rise stood The White Hare, a pale stone beacon shining in the darkness.

His lip curled, exposing the tips of his triple-bladed fangs. Fucking gorgeous, a tremendous piece of property located on the outskirts of Aberdeen, acreage he'd been trying to buy through legal channels for nearly two months. The Victorian mansion, with its wide windows, granite façade, and wildly pitched roofline, suited his tumultuous nature. So many angles. Too many chimneys. A cornucopia of extensions added over the centuries.

The mishmash of architectural styles never should've worked. Somehow though, it did—to stunning effect.

Once a popular playground for human elite (now the preferred one of Magickind visiting the area), the inn stood for everything he hated about humans. It was stalwart. It was welcoming and built to last. But it didn't know its place, refusing to crumble into dust, leaving history to languish alongside the location.

His temper sparked, making his black eyes glow in the gloom. Ruby shimmer rolled across the slate rooftop. Wood smoke from multiple chimneys swirled in his wake as he swung into a holding pattern, searching for the ideal place to land.

He eyed a narrow balcony, then shifted focus to the trees, shrubs, and vines in the back gardens. Probably best to set down in the tangled wood, away from the stone patio, and approach on foot instead of dragon paw.

Last time he visited, he'd played nice, given the innkeeper too much time, and ended up looking down the barrel of a shotgun. The ancient one Mavis brought with her from America.

He snorted. Toxic mist puffed from his nostrils then caught magical fire as he revolved into another turn. No matter how pretty the property, he should've shut Mavis down long before now. Why he continued negotiating with her, Kruger didn't know. The inherent challenge of besting her, maybe. The thrill of an honest win, perhaps. He couldn't say. Not really. No matter how much he turned the puzzle pieces over inside his mind, the reasons he continued to be gentle with her escaped him.

All he knew for certain was the stalemate had gone on too long.

So...

Time to do one of two things—speed up the process by scaring the shite out of her, or go with his gut, stick The White Hare on a spit, and roast the place.

Wouldn't take much: little more than a hiccup on his magical scale, and the fire-venom he commanded would devastate everything in its path.

His vicious side longed to do it, wanted to unleashed hell and watch the world burn.

Kruger tightened the hold on his beast's reins. Losing control wasn't a good idea.

As a hybrid, his magic crossed lines, allowing him to tap into multiple disciplines—earth, venomous, metallic, and fire dragon. He fit neatly into all four categories, wielding the skills of each Dragonkind subset without difficulty.

Rannock, his packmate and best friend, called his abilities majestic. If only his buddy knew the truth— the why behind all the power and how very different he was from others of their kind.

Not that he would ever tell his friend. Or anyone else, for that matter.

The mystery of who and what he was would go with him to the grave. Some secrets were meant to stay buried. The truth of his origins fit into that category, which sucked in ways he didn't enjoy thinking about. He hid a lot from his brothers-in-arms—lies by omission, a necessary deception with his life on the line.

With a sigh, Kruger picked his spot and folded his wings. Gravity yanked him out of the sky. Wind whistled over his scales. His paws slammed into disjointed flagstones. Fissures formed, cracking heavy rocks in half as a mini-earthquake shook the garden. Thick branches stretched wide, ancient trees swayed. The faded awning hanging from a neglected greenhouse rattled. With a murmur, he shut down the clamor, preferring stealth to full-frontal assault, and turned his attention to the mansion visible through the thicket.

Crouched low, he crept around the end of a hedgerow. The pads of his paws left flagstone underfoot. His claws scraped over compact dirt. The smell of old leaves and rich loam rose. Powerful magic followed, curling up from the earth, making his muscles twitch and his senses sing.

And he had his answer—the reason he hesitated to raze the place. The spirit of old earth lived here—the power of the ancient ones. Tales of centuries gone by were embedded deep, enriching the soil, feeding the land, making the earth dragon in him want to bed down and stay awhile.

Taking a deep breath, Kruger closed his eyes. By the goddess, he loved it here, in the gardens, beneath the trees, in a place so rich with magic he struggled to know where he stopped and the property began. The beauty of the Parkland's acceptance rattled around inside him, soothing the tattered edges of his soul.

A huge problem given what he planned.

One he didn't want to face as he shifted from dragon to human form. He hit his haunches without conjuring his clothes. Modesty be damned. He needed to make sure he was alone. Truly *alone*.

With Mavis's magical menagerie wandering about, even a Dragonkind warrior couldn't be sure he went undetected. The guests who came and went from The White Hare owned a variety of abilities. Not many Magickind could see through the cloaking spell he conjured, but...

No sense tempting fate. He wanted to surprise Mavis, not broadcast his arrival.

Balanced on the balls of his feet, Kruger stayed still and silent, becoming part of the landscape, absorbing the night sounds, enjoying the splash of the enormous fountain a hundred feet away. Inching forward, he scanned the rear of the hotel, then glanced toward the water feature positioned between the wide stone patio at the back of the house and the forest he hid inside.

Circular in shape, almost as large as an Olympic swimming pool, the fountain featured a statue of Poseidon, trident held high, rising from the froth of a curling sea at its center. Listening for telltale signs, Kruger watched the raised marble lip, waiting to see if—

Splashing sounded.

Laughter followed as three water nymphs surfaced in the fountain, splashing, giggling, frolicking in the moonlight. He watched the trio grab the smooth stone lip and kick out of the pool—two dark-skinned, one light, all with curvy bodies shielded by the wet fall of long, thick hair.

Gathering the gloom, he faded deeper into the shadows. Unaware of his proximity, the nymphs toweled off and, rounding the fountain edge, trotted up wide-mouthed stairs and across the patio. The hiss of hinges stroked through the quiet as the door opened and Mavis's major-domo stepped out. The pungent scent of gorgon assaulted Kruger's senses. He bit down on a snarl, watching as the half-man, half-snake—with dreadlocks instead of serpents for hair—slithered outside. Bowing his dark head, he waved an elegant hand, ushering the nymphs inside.

The trio giggled and hustled through the open door.

Pausing mid-slither, the gorgon scanned the back terrace. He hesitated, shimmering yellow eyes searching. Wrapped inside the cloaking spell, Kruger stared back, waiting for the moment the major-domo sensed his presence and—

The male turned away and followed his guests inside.

The collection of voices faded.

Kruger released a long, slow breath, then glared at the backside of the closed door. The stout oak surface mocked him with its pleasing shade of blue. Goddamn Mavis and her flair for hospitality. Everything about The White Hare screamed, *Welcome! Come in and stay awhile.*

He scowled.

Rocketing overhead, Levin snorted. Static blew into Kruger's head as a link opened into mind-speak. *"Seriously?"*

"Donnae start."

"We're Dragonkind. Top of the food chain. What would the gorgon have done—hissed at you? Stuck his forked tongue out and—"

"Lev—"

"And you're hiding in the thicket."

Kruger growled a warning.

His friend chuckled. *"And the innkeeper? She's, like,*

what...a hundred and two years old?"

"Seventy-three, arsehole."

"Whatever," Levin said. *"Huge threat, lad. Real big."*

"I'm not afraid of—"

"She's beating you at yer own game, mon."

Kruger tipped his head back to glare at his brother-in-arms. Fuck. He should've gone with his gut, snuck out of the lair, and left Levin at home. But Cyprus's decree that no one flew out alone had made him hesitate, then toe the line. A wise decision, no matter how much Levin annoyed him. With the Danish pack circling, attacking at random, the shift in protocol was a necessary one.

No one wanted to be caught out by the enemy pack. Which made accepting a wingmate a smart move, though he wished Rannock was at his back tonight. His best friend might be volatile, vicious, and impatient, but at least the male knew when to keep his mouth shut. Always the better bet when on mission. But with Cate now in the fold, Rannock was off rotation, taking a much-needed break to *play* with his mate. Something about tearing apart a classic car and putting the rust bucket back together.

"Ruger," Levin said, using Kruger's nickname.

Kruger clenched his teeth. *"What would you have me do—fry her?"*

"Thought that was the plan."

"In the beginning, mayhap."

"What happened?"

"She tried tae kill me."

"With what?"

"A shotgun. Vintage. Mint condition."

Levin laughed. *"She's got style. I think I like the old bird."*

Kruger thought he might too. Another problem to

add to the pile. A massive one that told him he might be losing his mind.

He never backed down. *Ever*. He won in the business world...period. He'd been involved in countless mergers and acquisitions, hostile takeovers and startups. Every business venture he touched turned to gold. His packmates—the warriors he lived with inside the underground lair beneath the Dragon's Horn —loved him for it. Mavis, however, had yet to see his appeal.

She upped the ante at every turn, making him want to tear his horns off. But after seven weeks battling with her, he'd come to know his opponent. Now, even as the situation surrounding The White Hare went from not-good to critical, he couldn't bring himself to end her life. Putting her in the ground left a bad taste in his mouth.

Somewhere along the way, he'd developed a soft spot for the aging female. For a human, she took surly to new heights. He should know: before meeting the shotgun-loving maniac, he thought he'd cornered the market on assholery. The innkeeper, however, created a new category, refusing to back down no matter how much pressure he put on her.

An epic tug of war. She yanked. He pulled. No ground was ever won.

Every time he talked to his solicitors, Kruger gave them new instructions, changing tactics, hoping to find one that worked. He played nice in the beginning, doubling his proffer *twice*, offering more than the pile of stones she called a hotel was worth, and yet...

He got nowhere. Which made no sense. Mavis O'-Donnell shouldn't be an obstacle—not for him.

The types of deals he brokered on a regular basis framed his interests. The why of a venture rarely mattered. He worked until he got what he wanted, so her refusal to sell tripped his trigger. He'd gone head-to-head with CEOs of powerful corporations—skilled negotiators and savvy businessmen the world over—who possessed less staying power than the human currently mucking up his plans.

"Annoying," he growled under his breath.

Ice-blue scales flashing moonlight, Levin hovered over the rooftop. His friend's midnight blue claws touched down, curling over the eaves without making a sound.

Folding his wings, Levin leveled his gaze on Kruger. *"Admit it—you admire her."*

"Do not." Deny. Obfuscate. Misdirect. Three excellent strategies, ones Kruger deployed often. *"She's a pain in the arse."*

"Admit it, Ruger. You like her."

"Go home, Lev."

"And miss all the fun? No way in hell."

"Stay out of my business."

"When have I ever done that?"

Never. The nosy male insisted on knowing everything. *"The right tae privacy—ever heard of it?"*

"We live inside a pack, mon. You kissed yer right tae privacy goodbye decades ago."

True. Still—frustrating as all fucking hell.

Pushing from his crouch, Kruger conjured his clothes. Jeans and a t-shirt settled on his skin. Motorcycle boots on his feet, he shrugged on his favorite leather jacket. *"I'm going in tae talk some sense into her. Donnae follow me."*

Levin huffed. *"Like that's gonna happen."*

With a sigh, Kruger stepped out from behind the hedge. A quick pace took him across the open area, around the huge fountain, and up the steps. His footfalls rapped inside the cloaking spell. He ignored the faint echo and crossed the patio toward the—

The door whipped open.

Kruger stopped.

Levin cursed and left his perch. The beat of wings sounded. Dragon paws thumped down on the terrace behind him. The potted plants sitting on the cobble-stones jumped. Ceramic clanked. Ice-cold air puffed against his nape, then chiseled down his spine.

Kruger didn't bother to glance over his shoulder. Fighting stance set, sonar up and running, he knew where his packmate stood—at his back, ice dragon out in full force, magic frothing, casting a long shadow as the gorgon exited the mansion.

Yellow eyes with green vertical pupils swept over Kruger without seeing him.

Gaze narrowed, he debated a moment. Throw the male a bone, make him work for it, or...

He rolled his shoulders. The illusion around him tore open. Kruger stepped out of the invisibility spell. The gorgon sucked in a quick breath. Fear flared in his eyes. Kruger stayed still, allowing the male to look at him, conveying an unspoken message—he wasn't here for him. He wanted something else. Something he'd been working toward for weeks—a private sit-down with the human who stood in his way.

Straightening his shoulders, the male recovered fast. Moving past shock, he slithered toward Kruger instead of away. Red, brown, and black scales rasped over cobblestones.

The male stopped less than ten feet away. Brave, considering whom he faced and why.

The gorgon inclined his head, showing him re-spect. "Master Kruger, I presume?"

"Aye," he murmured, focus riveted on Mavis's major-domo. "And you are?"

"Hendrix."

Kruger nodded. "I need a moment with your mistress."

"I understand, but I'm afraid that is quite impossible."

His temper spiked. Green fire-venom flickered over his shoulders. The smell of toxic fumes puffed in the air.

Hendrix flinched. "I can explain."

"Good idea," Kruger said, unable to keep the snarl from his tone.

Levin uncloaked behind him. Magic crackled across stone, leaving a thick layer of frost in its wake.

"Gods," Hendrix breathed, gaze bouncing from him to Levin. "My apologies, sir, but you are too late. The innkeeper is no longer in residence. She has retired."

Levin bared his fangs. "What the fuck does that mean?"

"Dead?" Kruger asked at the same time.

"No, sir. Retired. As in—"

"Bloody hell," he growled, losing patience. "Where is she?"

"Acapulco, I believe."

Kruger blinked.

"You have got tae be shitting me," Levin grumbled, pushing from a low crouch. His dragon scales clicked as he powered up, dragging the temperature into single digits. Snow started to fall. "A ploy."

The gorgon shivered.

Kruger bared his teeth. A wave of heat rolled into the air. Snowflakes melted as his temper went from a low simmer to a boil. "'Twas planned. All the delays. The constant couching. She played me."

Hendrix took a fortifying breath. "I cannot say, sir, but—"

"Or refused to."

"Sir?"

"Never mind." Kruger could guess what came next. He wasn't a fool. Neither was Mavis. She excelled in the strategic arena. No way would she exit the battlefield without a parting shot. The innkeeper liked war too much to leave her opponent unscathed. Which meant he must look beyond Hendrix to see the mess Mavis had left for him in her wake. "What did she do?"

"She asked me to give you this." Reaching into the breast pocket of his velvet tuxedo jacket, Hendrix withdrew a crisp white envelope. Thin, plain paper. Nothing fancy about it.

Which told Kruger all he needed to know—he was about to get screwed with his pants on.

Bowing his head, the gorgon offered the letter.

Kruger took it, then murmured. Magic rushed to do his bidding, slicing the top of the sealed envelope open. Paper crinkled as he withdrew the single sheet. He broke the wax seal stamped with an olive branch.

He snorted. Seriously? *An olive branch.* He had to give her credit. The old bat never ceased to surprise him. She owned the most twisted sense of humor around.

"What does it say?" Icy breath fogging the air, Levin peered over his shoulder.

Fingers itching, Kruger flipped open the trifold. A messy scrawl written by a shaky hand. A couple of golden grains of sand stuck to the crest of The White Hare letterhead.

. . .

Kruger,

I told you I would never sell. You didn't believe me. In a word—foolish.

The White Hare has been in my family for centuries. We are the caretakers of Magickind, the ones who stand in the breech. The inn is not for sale, and never will be.

I win.

You lose.

Good luck with the next innkeeper, dragon. Her will is much stronger than mine.

Sincerely (and fuck you),
Mavis O'Donnell
The innkeeper, retired.

His brow furrowed, Kruger stared at her departing line. His lips twitched. It wasn't funny. Given the gravity, nothing about the situation came anywhere near laughable, but...shite. He admired her spirit, liked her creativity, along with the audacity of her final *fuck you*.

Not many butted up against Dragonkind and lived to talk about it. But Mavis had, sending him on a wild goose chase before she walked away, leaving him tangled up in the mess she'd left him with true maniacal intent.

He liked her style. He really did, though...

The next innkeeper.

"Bloody hell," Levin growled. "What now?"

What now, indeed? Excellent question.

Magic sparking, Kruger's eyes started to shimmer. Crimson bled over white paper as he closed the letter and stared at the olive branch. Another *fuck you*, boldly stamped in broken green wax. Running the pad of his thumb over the crest, assessing his options, Kruger listened to the gorgon murmur "goodnight" and retreat into the inn.

He glanced over his shoulder. Pale snowy eyes met his. Levin raised a brow. Kruger smiled. Not a pleasant, all-is-right-in-my-world one, but a nasty, venom-filled one.

"Yikes." Claws scraped over stone as his friend took two giant steps backward. "Whoever the new one is, she's fucked."

Wasn't she, though? No wiggle room for the newly anointed innkeeper.

Kruger needed to purchase The White Hare for more reasons than he'd let on. Forget about his affinity for the Parkland; toss aside the fact the acquisition would protect his pack by shielding the new tunnel he'd dug from the Cairngorms into the Aberdeen lair, ensuring it went undetected by other Magickind. For that reason alone, dropping millions to buy the inn was worth the aggravation.

Another reason—one more sinister and less altruistic—existed. A reason that landed closer to home... and his own heart.

Having Magickind around was dangerous. Not to the Scottish pack, but for him. His secret was a fragile one, a carefully constructed mirage that would disappear if one of the elder races came to stay at The White Hare. He or she might recognize him, seek him out to pay homage, reveal what he tried so hard to keep hidden—force him to face his packmates and the consequences of concealing his true origins.

The instant Cyprus and the others learned the truth, he'd be exiled. Mayhap even killed for hiding his bloodline.

Kruger clenched his teeth. His fucking father. The male's stink followed him everywhere he went.

It didn't matter that he'd never met the irresponsible arsehole. The damage Silfer had done to Dragonkind couldn't be undone. The fallout would never stop. After centuries of suffering, his race's struggle went on ad infinitum. Each generation passed the curse on to the next, siring males who lacked the ability to connect to the Meridian and draw nourishment from the electrostatic bands ringing the planet, providing what a warrior needed to stay healthy and strong.

His sire had done that—betraying the Goddess of All Things along with those he represented in the Heavenly Realm by impregnating a wood nymph... and siring him.

Kruger's chest tightened. So much fucking pain. All that upheaval. Goddess, what his mother must've suffered bringing him into the world. He could hardly wrap his brain around it—or his sire's selfishness. The hubris floored him. The continued struggle of Dragonkind made his heart hurt. Nothing he did would repair the damage.

The connection lay shattered, beyond help or repair. So aye...

No way around it.

He would never tell anyone where he came from —or who'd sired him. Heartache along with certain death lay in that direction, which left him one option —no more playing nice with humans.

He would wait for the new innkeeper to show up and do what must be done: eliminate her fast, take what he wanted instead of negotiating for what he needed. The White Hare wouldn't be under new management long. He'd make sure of it.

2

CHICAGO, ILLINOIS

Every once in a while, life threw you a bone. Ferguson McGilvery remembered those days, when everything was golden, shiny, and bright. Before the wounds deepened and pain crept in from the edges, making things turn from good to bad. She longed for the days when life set its thumb on the scales, landing on her side instead of throwing curveballs—ones she never managed to hit.

It was the damnedest thing, those strikeouts. Her batting average had always been solid. Never one thousand, mind you, but a respectable eighty percent at least.

Strange the things one took for granted while sailing on good vibes through a smooth patch—like stable relationships and financial security.

Despite her skill at playing the odds (statistics had always been her jam), she hadn't seen it coming. She'd been too trusting, an idiot each and every way she sliced it. The facts weren't in dispute. The worst-case scenario had arrived with a thunderclap, knocking her off her cozy perch.

An elaborate illusion, conjured by a master of deception.

Her husband had created the bubble, then wrapped her inside it. And she'd stayed oblivious, wasting seven years of her life with a man she believed loved her.

Seven years.

Seven freaking years.

Ferguson couldn't believe she'd fallen for the ruse, or that she still struggled to let go of the dream. Everything was upside down and backward, twisted in a way she couldn't straighten out, and most days didn't want to, though sometimes...

Swiveling away from her computer screen, she tipped her chair back. Hinges creaked. Stained ceiling tiles looked down on her. She stared back at the messy collection, then frowned. Seemed like a metaphor for her life right now. Hanging on by a thread, about to come down around her, ratty beyond repair.

Concentrating on a yellow stain above her head, Ferguson scowled, not wanting to admit she longed for the good old days. A foolish reaction. Doing what her ex wanted, returning to the dysfunction, sounded as crazy as it was, but...

All that golden, shiny, and bright was seductive in the midst of upheaval. Human nature, maybe— longing for the familiar. To return to the known, no matter how screwed up, instead of forging new paths into the wilderness that had become her life.

Going back, however, wasn't an option. Four months changed a lot. Not much time in the grand scheme of things, but plenty enough for everything to slide downhill. No way of slowing down, never mind bring the careening calamity to a halt.

She'd face-planted. Spectacularly, in public, losing her mind when she found out...and everything else shortly thereafter. Which landed her here, in the last place she wanted to be—the family business (the one her mother married into), working alongside her step-brothers.

Pressing the balls of her feet into the floor, Ferguson rolled her chair farther away from her cubicle. Rubber wheels rasped over carpet. A clunk sounded behind her.

The surfer-dude voice came next. "Feeling sorry for yourself again?"

With a sigh, she closed her eyes. Why her? Why now? Why couldn't everyone just leave her the hell alone?

She glanced over her shoulder. "You're early."

Bleach-blond hair in a messy halo around his head, Jethro stepped on the edge of his skateboard. The wheels flipped up into his hand. Dark brows popped over ocean-blue eyes, heading toward his forehead. "Dude, I'm fucking vapor. You expect me to keep track of time?"

She sighed again. So much for common courtesy. Jethro—next-level surfer, pothead bohemian—never cared what she thought. Or that she didn't want him around during office hours.

For good reason, too.

He was dead, as in—no longer among the *living*, breathing normal human beings she interacted with every day.

No one else but her could see him, which put her in a whole other category. One her mother had called *special*, and Ferguson called screwed up. Being the go-between, communing with the spirit world, sucked. Not that anyone wanted to hear her opinion.

Keeping with Jethro's ongoing theme, none of her visitors cared she wanted nothing to do with them. Ghosts came and went, showing up in her space, scaring the shit out of her on a regular basis. Though since what she liked to call *the catastrophe*, and the subsequent dismantling of her life, only Jethro and Cuthbert (the English butler who drowned in a pond trying to save a cat during the Victorian Age) popped in to chat.

Or rather, checked up on her. Their way of describing the crazy-ass visits, not hers.

"People already think I'm nuts, Jethro." Ignoring the mountain of file folders growing like fungus on her desktop, she swung around in her chair. "You trying to give them more ammunition?"

"Who cares what these assholes think?" He treated her to a pointed look, then flipped a joint into his mouth. A cheap plastic lighter flamed, and the pungent scent of weed hit her, ramping her irritation into double digits, given no one but her could smell it. "Partake of the green goddess and chill the fuck out, Fergie."

His answer for everything.

He blew out a stream of smoke.

She wrinkled her nose. "You mind?"

"Nope. No one else does either." His brow furrowed. "Where the fuck is everyone?"

"Lunch."

"And you're still here? Instead of outside in the sun? Fuck, you could be at the skate park or—"

"I don't board."

"Down by the water. Got that sweet kite sitting in a box in your apartment. Could be outside flying it instead of in here fucking up your life."

Crossing her arms over her chest, she scowled at him.

He huffed. "Seriously, dude. What the hell?"

"Unlike you, I've got loads of work to—"

"Now you're acting like one of these assholes. Total worker-bee mentality."

"Jethro—"

"Get with the program, Fergie. Fuck the establishment. Get out and *live*."

"Gotta eat, man."

"You open your mind, and the world will open up for you," he said, taking another toke, getting baked while delivering his surfer-dude life philosophy. "You don't need this job. You don't need this shit. You don't—"

A door slammed across the office.

"Ferguson—hey," Darren called, interrupting Jethro. "Good, you're still here."

Her stepbrother's voice raked across already raw nerve endings. Footfalls tapped across carpet, heading in her direction.

Ferguson drew a fortifying breath, then spun her chair away from Jethro. Her gaze collided with Darren's over the half wall protecting her cubicle. A sea of boring beige stood beyond it. Plain doors into private offices (some open, others closed) bookended a conference room with fancy furniture bought to impress high-end clients. The open section she worked in, full of gray cubicles and drab olive chairs, provided a clear line of sight across an office that screamed minimalistic and modern. The view didn't improve as Darren approached her little patch of heaven, arm curled around a stack of folders.

"Great," Jethro grumbled behind her. "Fuckwad number one inbound."

She bit down on a snort. Years of practice smoothed her expression into neutral lines. The lesson was burned into her brain—never reveal her odd ability. Never let on she was rarely alone. Accept the strange looks people in her immediate proximity treated her to when the spirit world interrupted her own, and she ended up looking like she was talking to herself in a room full of people.

No one but her mother and Mavis knew the truth. Myriam McGilvery had insisted her daughter stayed hidden. Mavis, Ferguson's godmother, agreed, helping her mother move from Scotland to America when the extent of her abilities became clear...just after Ferguson turned three.

Watching Darren traverse the open-plan office, she pushed to her feet. The chair creaked in protest. She ignored the complaint. Time for a coffee break, and maybe some Valium. Not that she ever took the stuff. Drugs weren't the answer. Murder, maybe, given her stepbrother's attitudes, but prescription meds numbed her mind.

Blunting her abilities never ended well for the *In-between*—the space between the living world and the afterlife. Without her internal guards up, functioning at optimal capacity, a gateway could open, altering the spirit realm along with the earthly one. Not good for anyone, living or dead.

She'd done it once in college. A pissed-off poltergeist ended up haunting her dorm for months before she managed to coax it back where it belonged. To its happy place—the underworld.

Dressed to kill in an expensive suit, Darren stopped outside her cubicle. "Listen, I need you to—"

"Greetings, fuckwad," Jethro said, even though Darren couldn't hear him.

"No," she said at the same time.

Her stepbrother blinked. "What?"

"Not gonna happen. Not this time...or the next."

Nothing but a golden, hazy outline, Jethro freed up

his hands by shoving the joint in his mouth. Smoke clouding the air around him, he clapped. "Thatta girl."

Darren shifted the folders he carried from one hand to cradle the stack in two. "Dad needs these by tomorrow morning, and—"

"Do it yourself, Darren."

"I've got—"

"What—another client meeting at Bo Jangles?"

His expression went from "beseeching puppy dog" to hard lines. "You don't know what you're talking about."

"Don't I?"

She eyed the folders, most of which didn't belong to her, stacked in haphazard piles on her desk. Her purview included payroll and HR. She was good at her job, making sure everyone who worked at Taylor & Co. got what they deserved—a regular paycheck and pleasant working conditions. The work her stepbrothers dumped on her desk was theirs, not hers, and honestly? One more file, and her cubicle would collapse inward, spewing debris all over the office.

Pursing her lips, she took a moment to mourn her love of all things organization, then glared at Darren.

Her stepbrothers were getting ridiculous. Again. Taking advantage, pushing boundaries. Spending more time outside the office than in it, expecting her to pick up the slack.

Some things never changed.

Every day, the same argument—dustups she might win in the moment, but always lost in the end. The super brats always did what they pleased despite her objections, dumping their responsibilities in her lap.

She stayed late most days to get all the work done, but Darren and Dillon employed the hit-and-run method: drop their work on her desk or inbox and duck out fast, only to arrive the next day with excuses —something urgent, in need of their immediate attention. A dinner with clients to smooth over a complaint. Drinks with a business contact to ensure the next contract came through. Golf with industry professionals to network and keep the pipeline full.

None of it true.

She'd seen the expense reports and knew where they went—Bo Jangles, the swankiest strip club in town. An obvious favorite of the Taylors, given her stepfather never blinked an eye. He signed off on the expenses, allowing his sons to run amuck.

Raking her hands through her hair, Ferguson stripped the elastic band off her wrist. A couple of quick twists put the thick strands in a ponytail. What had she been thinking? She never should've come back and ought to be long gone by now. No way should she be allowing history to repeat itself. The second the super brats slid into old patterns, she should've walked into her stepfather's fancy corner office and said, "I'm outta here."

She told herself to do it every day, gave herself resounding pep talks on a regular basis. In her car before walking through the front doors. During lunch at her desk while wading through an avalanche of paperwork. On her way home in the dark after picking up takeout.

Something needed to change.

And lately, she kept thinking the thing that needed to change was *her*. She was the problem, the one unwilling to do the necessary thing, the sane thing, the brave thing—buck up, take the bullet, walk away, and never look back.

Problem was...

The balance in her bank account stated she

needed the money. She hadn't lied to Jethro. A girl needed to eat, preferably beneath the roof she paid rent to keep over her head.

Independence took work, a lot of it. She'd achieved it once, but let it go when she got married. Why? Good question. One Ferguson couldn't answer without feeling foolish. She'd trusted Brent, seen forever in his eyes instead of searching for the kind of substance that bred loyalty. Now, everything seemed hard. She had a mountain of debt to climb and a list of *must-do*s a mile long.

First things first, though...

No more Mrs. Nice Girl.

Her stepbrothers needed to learn she wasn't a dumping ground. Or a doormat. Being the workhorse in a business that called her family, but treated her like the help, wasn't the way to go.

Obviously. And yet she felt stuck, paralyzed by uncertainty and terrified of the unknown.

Her mother would be so disappointed.

The thought made her sick to her stomach. She needed to print off the resignation letter she wrote last week, sign the damn thing, and hand it to her stepfather.

Pronto. Before fear got the better of her, and she stayed in a situation that would eventually crush her soul.

"Nice attitude," Darren said, a nasty glint in his eyes. "Thought you needed this job?"

Jethro took a step toward him.

She held out her hand, stalling her ghost-maybe-only-friend midstride. She didn't need the added aggravation. Jethro might not be able to touch Darren, but that didn't mean he couldn't hurt him. Heavy things tended to fall off high shelves onto unsuspecting heads with a pissed-off ghost around.

Her eyes narrowed. "Are you threatening me?"

"I'm your boss. I put it on your desk; you do the work. Just like before. Just like always. Don't think you can—"

"I can. I'm not taking any more crap from you. Or anyone else."

"Fuck the establishment!" Jethro yelled, and started clapping again.

Darren set the file folders down on her desk with a thump. An already too-high pile cascaded into an avalanche, burying her keyboard. "Do it, or kiss your paycheck goodbye."

"I'm gonna kill him." Eyes narrowed, Jethro twisted the end off his joint, then flicked it toward Darren. The invisible ember hit her stepbrother in the cheek.

"Ow!" Darren jerked, wiped at his face, then glanced at the ceiling. "What the hell?"

She sent Jethro a pointed look.

Wavy blond hair hanging in his eyes, he cracked his knuckles. "Say the word, bro, and he's toast. I'll—"

"Don't tempt me," she said to Jethro while glaring at Darren.

Her stepbrother scowled, opened his mouth, no doubt to say something insulting, and—

"Ms. McGilvery?"

Her attention snapped to her right.

Bridget, the new receptionist, stood five feet from the edge of her cubicle. Young, pretty, shy, a sophomore in college home for the summer. A girl ripe for the slaughter. Just the kind of bright-eyed innocent Darren and Dillon liked to hire.

Ferguson's stomach dropped. God help her. She

needed to have a chat with the newest employee at Taylor & Co. Otherwise, her stepbrothers would chew Bridget up, spit her out, then move on to more challenging prey.

Wide eyes bouncing between her and Darren, Bridget cleared her throat. "Ah…"

"You need me?" Ferguson asked, watching the girl shuffle from foot to foot.

"There's a"—Bridget bit her bottom lip—"man here to see you."

"A man?"

"A lawyer. From the U.K."

Ferguson blinked. "The U.K.?"

Odd, but not unheard of in Chicago. Lots of law firms had offices in the United Kingdom and employees who traveled between the two countries.

Bridget nodded. "He doesn't have an appointment, but refuses to leave. Says it's urgent, absolutely *vital* he speak with you."

Ferguson quelled the urge to roll her eyes. She just bet the guy refused to leave. Not a surprise, given the nastiness of the divorce proceedings and the legal roadblocks Brent continued to put in her way.

"Dude," Jethro muttered. "I hate your dweeb of a husband."

"Ex," she said, correcting the record, making Bridget and Darren throw her strange looks.

Par for the course. Everyone thought she was odd. And for the most part, she *was*—weird in ways no one but the ghosts who visited her would ever understand.

"I'll handle it, Bridget."

"Ferguson," Darren half growled, half whined, "we're not done talking about—"

"Yes, we are." Shoulders squared, Ferguson rounded the edge of her cubicle. "Pick up your folders and screw off, Darren. You leave it there, it won't get done."

"Wait just a minute. I need—"

"Go away." Glaring at her stepbrother, she marched past Taylor & Co.'s new receptionist. "Where did you put him?"

"Small conference room next to reception," Bridget said, hightailing it after her.

Ferguson nodded. "Perfect."

A lie. Nothing was *perfect*. It hadn't been for a while. Would never be again, which meant...

Time to take the bull by the horns.

First step—dispatch the lawyer her ex-husband had no doubt sent to stall the divorce proceedings. Second order of business—hand her letter of resignation to her holier-than-thou-do-what-I-say-not-what-I-do stepfather. After that, she planned to take Jethro's advice, find some Zen, and get some sun by taking a walk in the mother-effing park.

The trip overseas felt as though it lasted forever.

Planes. Trains. And automobiles. Not that the method of transportation or time frame mattered. Not to Ferguson.

Leaving Chicago and the mess she'd made of her life was no hardship. The difficult part began and ended with the unknown, with her imagination and the questions running riot through her mind. What would she find? Would it feel like home? Or had the faded memories she carried become distorted into an idealized version of what had once been—of what she wanted the past to be?

She'd asked all those questions on the plane, then repeated each one on the train out of London. Seven hours spent looking out the window at the country-side while the locomotive chugged north toward the Scottish Highlands. Almost twenty-nine years to the day after her mother picked up and left Aberdeen.

Her recall was sketchy. Long hours spent traveling didn't provide any clues to the mystery of that night, beyond the fact she was going home.

The realization crystallized the moment she'd stepped inside Taylor & Co.'s smallest conference

room and saw who waited for her. Dressed in a suit
that cost more than her car, the man had oozed
charisma. Not unusual for a lawyer, especially the
ones her ex-husband liked to hire, but the guy was unlike anyone she'd ever seen.

Tall. Built. Blunt features. Something odd about
the color of his eyes. Throw in thick eyebrows, bushy
sideburns, and a scruffy beard into the mix of lethality
he wore like an overcoat and...yeah, he'd captured her
attention immediately. She'd kept her focus on him as
she closed the door behind her. A soft click echoed in
the conference room. The soft buzz of halogens
picked up the slack, piercing the quiet as she looked at
him and he looked back, studying her like an ento-
mologist would a bug.

She remained silent.

He didn't say a word.

The air took on an ethereal quality, fogging the space
around him. Her skin prickled. Intuition needled into
her like driving rain. Cold calculation turned to warm
welcome as something innate rose, providing her with
information. *Other. Different.* Not in the way she was, but
she understood the complexity of his nature without
asking—and knew exactly how to deal with him.

With authority, courage, and unwavering resolve.

Holding his gaze, she raised a brow, prompting
him.

When he didn't take the hint, she crossed her arms
and waited. How she found the strength in the face of
his unspoken aggression, Ferguson didn't know. Tiny
threads merged inside her, weaving a primal pattern,
knitting understanding together, allowing instinct to
lead.

One side of his mouth curved up. "You'll do."

"Good to know," she said, sounding unaffected when she felt anything but. Heartbeat throbbing in her throat, she moved farther into the room. A bold move, given his size. Everything about the guy screamed big—the width of his shoulders, the strength of his hands, the caliber of his character. She pulled the name Bridget gave her from the back of her brain. "How may I help you, Mr. Montague?"

"It's Montague, my dear—just Montague, no mister," he said with a British accent. Not crisp enunciation, but flat, rounded vowels. More Cockney, less upper-crust London.

"Okay."

"And you are Ms. McGilvery."

"I am."

"Ferguson McGilvery?"

She nodded.

"Then I've come to the right place."

"You were in doubt?"

"No."

"Then why—"

"Unimportant." He withdrew a stack of papers from inside a beat-up leather briefcase with brusque efficiency and slapped the pile down on the table. "I don't have a lot of time. The full moon is tonight, and I must make proper preparations."

Full moon? Preparations?

She frowned. Her ex must be desperate if he was stuck hiring weird-ass lawyers worried about phases of the moon. "Listen, I already told Brent what I want. It's all written down in the—"

He tapped the paperwork with his fingertip, one tipped with a long nail filed into a sharp point. The thing looked lethal, if somewhat impractical. An odd choice of manicure for a man. An even weirder one for a lawyer.

"You remember your godmother?" he asked, raising a bushy brow.

"Mavis?"

"Yes."

"Of course," she said, her voice strained.

She remembered everything about her mother's best friend. The letters Mavis sent once a month—handwritten on fancy letterhead with an even fancier crest—kept her tied to Scotland and the life she'd left behind...one she would never lead. Her mother made her promise—over and over—not to visit until the time was right.

It's all in the timing, my beautiful girl. Something her mother had said often, just another cryptic message that never made much sense.

And yet she'd done what her mother wanted—stayed away. Instinct, maybe. A sense of something unsafe, perhaps. Ferguson didn't know, but whatever the reason, she'd made a life in America while looking forward to Mavis's letters each month. In some strange way, the sheets of paper with perfect, looping scrawl had become her lifeline, a way to hold on to the memory of her mother after she died. The tie that reminded her who she was and that she'd once belonged...somewhere.

"How is she?"

"Mavis?" Flipping through the pages, Montague shrugged. "Well, I hope."

"You hope?"

"Having fun in the sun."

"What?"

"Last I heard, Acapulco. But that's neither here nor

there. Her location no longer matters—yours, however, does…a great deal, I'm afraid."

Her brows snapped together. "She—"

"Retired, a week ago, and has gifted you with everything. The White Hare, the Parkland, all of the accounts. Which means, you, my dear, are the new innkeeper."

"Innkeeper?"

"Exactly." A sparkle entered Montague's eyes. "Now, come over here. I need your signature in a number of places. After that, I'll ensure all is transferred into your name. I've taken the liberty of booking your flight, so…"

Her ears started ringing.

He kept talking. "Blah-blah-blah. And blah-blah. And also, blah."

She hadn't heard a thing after he said *booking your flight.* All she recalled were the dotted lines, the ones Montague pointed to where she signed her name.

Which brought her to where she sat now—in another country, in the back of an antique car with curled fenders and fancy running boards, being chauffeured by a *gorgon* to The White Hare.

Or, at least, she was pretty sure Hendrix was a gorgon.

"Check your binder." Stroking Luther, the black cat he'd died trying to save from a pond in Victorian England, Cuthbert glanced at her from the passenger seat.

"Meow," Luther said, agreeing.

Ferguson glanced at Hendrix.

Two hands on the wheel, he drove without batting an eye at the covert conversation. Which told her one of two things—either he didn't know he had company in the front seat, or he didn't care.

"The binder," Cuthbert said, pointing to the messenger bag in her lap.

She threw him an aggrieved look. "So bossy."

He raised a brow.

"And snooty. Never thought I'd say it, but I miss Jethro."

Cuthbert stuck his nose in the air. "That rapscallion? 'Tis a wonder he didn't go straight to Hell."

Luther purred in agreement.

With a sigh, she glanced down at her bag. No sense arguing with Cuthbert. He wouldn't leave her in peace until she checked. The guy might've been an English butler to an aristocratic family while alive, but he never met an argument he didn't like. Though you'd think, given his vocation, he'd be a little more polite.

Undoing the wide buckles, she flipped her bag open. Worn by years of use, scarred leather snagged at her fingertips. The satchel had once been a favorite of her mother's, now Ferguson's go-to accessory in stressful situations. She'd dragged the bag out of the back of her closet after signing the papers...and packing her suitcases. Seemed only fitting to bring the bag back to the place it had been made, the place it all began.

Reaching inside, she pulled out the binder Montague had handed her before wishing her luck and disappearing out the door. Inside, the title page read: *Udo's Quick Reference Guide to All Manner of Magical Creatures.* Under it, in parentheses: *For more detailed information, reference Udo's Master Manual of Magic Creatures, volumes I, II, III, IV & V.*

Seemed far-fetched, completely unbelievable, one hundred percent made up—until she stepped off the train in Aberdeen and saw Hendrix in all his half man, half snake glory.

Not that anyone else noticed. Passengers streamed around him. Employees manning the luggage line had smiled at him, nodded politely, and moved on to the next bag while she stood speechless (and Hendrix slithered away with her suitcases). She hadn't been able to make sense of him, still didn't know what to think as she watched him drive from the backseat.

Montague had tried to warn her, with a gentle voice—and a lot of understanding—as he gathered up the signed documents and handed her the binder.

Her hand slid over the front cover. Indentations and ridges pulled her fingertip across the crest stamped at its center, one representing The White Hare. Her godmother's hotel, the place Mavis wrote about in every letter, recounting tales from the Parkland, full of names, dates, and places.

Though none had ever mentioned *gorgons*. Or any of the other creatures she'd read about after cracking the binder open on the plane.

Inhaling deep, she looked out the side window. A clear, cloudless night crowned by a bright, faultless moon. The gentle glow painted the countryside with sliver strokes, allowing her to pick out landmarks in the dark. Hip-high stone fences hugged the narrow road, rambling by small cottages and barns, through wide-open fields and dense forest.

The car bumped over a rough patch. Her thoughts jagged along with it. So much had been kept from her.

The ghost angle she understood. Thanks to her mother, she accepted her gift most of the time, but everything else? Mavis and her mother should've told her about The White Hare, about its legacy and her role as heir. About becoming the next innkeeper.

She needed training. Lots of it.

Instead, she was going in cold, without the necessary knowledge required to manage what amounted to a hotel that welcomed those of a preternatural bent.

She wanted to be angry at her mother—and rail against Mavis. Memories rose instead, forcing her to remember the night everything changed.

Even at three years old, she'd known something was wrong—that her mother was surprised by something. She recalled her mother's face, the wild run, the constant checking over her shoulder, and realized *leaving* wasn't the right word. Myriam McGilvery had fled. In the middle of the night. With a small bag in one hand and Ferguson clutched tight in the other.

The mystery had always bothered her.

She'd asked...and asked, then asked some more. She never got any answers. But she recognized the playbook, the one her mother used when she didn't want to talk about something—deflection, obfuscation, and eventual silence on the subject.

Someday, my beautiful girl, you'll understand.

Her mother's favorite words. Another cryptic turn of phrase. So effing frustrating, given understanding never arrived. She'd been in the dark for three decades, muddling her way through life, trying to make sense of her gift, wondering what it meant—and what she was good for.

Her attention returned to the binder in her lap. Uncurling her fingers from around the edge, she opened the cover. Plastic crinkled as she flipped to the section labelled G.

"Hendrix?"

"Yes, my lady?"

Her lips pursed. *My lady.* Talk about kicking it old school. "It's Fergie, remember?"

"I remember."

"But you don't care. You'll continue to call me 'my lady' whether I like it or not."

"Of course."

"Why?"

"You're the innkeeper, my lady."

"Doesn't mean you can't call me by name." Thumbing the plastic corner, she turned a page, then another, working her way through the G section. Gorgon...gorgon...where the hell was the entry for gorgon? "And honestly, if I'm your boss, then I get to make the rules. Seems like this one is a good one to break."

His brow furrowed.

"Right?"

Citrine eyes with vertical pupils meet hers in the rearview mirror.

"I mean—no harm, no foul. New innkeeper, new way of looking at the world. Seems reasonable, don't you think?"

A horrified look winged across his face. The tips of his dreadlocks quivered. The car drifted off smooth pavement onto the rough shoulder. Gravel pinged against the undercarriage. Hendrix yanked the wheel. Springs squeaked as the antique car lurched back onto the road. "My la—"

"Great! Then it's decided," she said, smiling at him. "No more calling me *my lady*."

He blinked, but recovered fast. "As you wish, my liege."

"Seriously? You gonna run through every single one? What's next—laird?"

"Probably. So best to stop while you're ahead."

She rolled her eyes. "You're worse than Cuthbert."

The ghost in question sniffed. "I resent the implication."

"Shut up, Cuthbert."

"Meow," Luther said, defending his friend, green eyes fixed on her.

Hendrix blinked. "My liege?"

"Never mind." Trailing her finger down a page, Ferguson found the correct entry. She skimmed the information about gorgons. Top half man, bottom half serpent—check. Venomous snakes instead of hair—negative in Hendrix's case. The ability to drive without feet—huge question mark. "I've got a few questions."

"I'm available to answer all your questions—always, my liege—though perhaps your curiosity can wait until the morrow." Gaze trained on the road, Hendrix put his blinker on and made a left-hand turn. Tires crunched over gravel. He pressed a button on the dash. Heavy iron gates swung open, allowing him to drive between two enormous estate pillars. "We're here."

Shuffling toward the middle of the backseat, Ferguson peered through the windshield. Headlights ate through the gloom, sweeping over huge tree trunks. Planted at even intervals, oaks marched up the drive. Leafy canopies met and shook hands overhead, making it seem as though Hendrix drove through a living tunnel. She searched the darkness on either side of the winding lane, trying to get a sense of the terrain. Not much to see so late at night, but despite the thick shadows, she made out manicured flowerbeds and what looked like an expansive lawn beyond the tree line.

Light appeared at the top of the rise.

"There," Hendrix murmured, steering wide around a bend.

Her lips parted as she got her first look at The White Hare.

Pale stone façade lit up by a multitude of exterior lights, the five-story building looked to be part castle, part Victorian manor house. Some sections boasted square, toothy bulwarks. Other parts had peaked rooflines with stone inlay and turrets with round roofs. The hodgepodge of mismatched styles fit together with seamless beauty, the kind that no doubt made visitors stop and stare.

Ferguson wasn't immune. The graceful lines captivated her imagination as prickles swept the length of her spine. The odd tingle curled over her shoulders, then sank deep, unraveling the tight knot sitting in the center of her chest. She knew the tension well, had lived with it every day her entire life. From the moment she woke in the morning, intuition called, telling her she'd landed in wrong place, was lost out in the world, instead of where she belonged.

In Chicago, she sensed the disconnect...and always had. Something was wrong. Something was missing. Discordant in ways she couldn't explain or begin to understand.

She'd never been normal. The ghosts who visited day in and night out made that clear, but...

Closing her eyes, Ferguson breathed deep and settled into the sensation. Being here felt right. She was more than just needed. She was necessary and welcome, somehow vital to this place. She belonged even though she—

"Praise the goddess," Hendrix murmured.

"What?"

"Do you feel it?"

"Yes," she said, voice soft, eyes still closed, listening to the spirit of The White Hare whisper. "What's happening?"

"You are the rightful heir, my liege."

"I don't understand."

"You will," he whispered.

She opened her eyes.

Citrine eyes brimming with tears, Hendrix met her gaze in the rearview mirror. He smiled. "The White Hare welcomes you, my liege. Less than a minute on the property, and the bond is already forming. With you here, the inn will soon return to full health, to her former glory, and we will enjoy full occupancy once more."

He sounded thrilled by the prospect.

Ferguson frowned. "You need to explain what just happened."

"It is not my place. When you are ready, the Parkland will introduce itself."

"That doesn't make any sense. How am I supposed to—"

"Patience, my liege. All will be revealed in due time."

In due time. Sounded like the title of a bad soap opera. One she wanted no part in.

"Patience isn't my forte, Hendrix."

He chuckled. "Never too late to start learning some."

"Excellent advice," Cuthbert said, snotty tone out in full force. "How long have I been telling you that?"

"God save me," she grumbled, skewering the butler with a nasty look before turning it on the gorgon. Her glare bounced right off him.

Clenching her teeth, Ferguson slammed the binder closed. Hendrix's smile turned into a grin. She scowled at him, then decided to let it go...for now. Arguing with the gorgon wouldn't get her anywhere. He was entrenched, convinced his way was the best way, so... time to put her business hat on and get into the nitty-gritty. All the pesky details she needed to know in order to run the inn and turn a profit.

"How many rooms inside the inn?"

"Not rooms, my liege—suites."

"How many?"

"Sixty-seven," Hendrix said, maneuvering around a fountain featuring three stags, twisted manes flying, front hooves rearing. Bare-chested warriors sat on their backs, swords raised high, faces twisted in maniacal lines. "Though some guests prefer to stay in the stables."

"The stables," Cuthbert muttered with disdain.

She threw him a warning glance. The last thing she needed was more of his opinions—or to deal with the butler's hoity-toity standards. Later would be soon enough to listen to him grumble about propriety and the way things *ought to be done* in a proper household.

"Sixty-seven," she murmured, wondering what The White Hare pulled in each year. The revenue must be healthy, much more interesting than Taylor & Co.'s. The tips of her fingers began to itch. God, the fun. She could hardly wait to crack the books open and take a look. She loved numbers, enjoyed accounting and doing a business planning (much to Jethro's frustration and Cuthbert's everlasting delight) more than baseball fanatics loved statistics.

"Not including your private flat."

She blinked. "I have an apartment?"

"Of course, my liege. A very beautiful one, as befitting your station."

"You make me sound like royalty."

"To us, you are."

Cuthbert perked up at the news. Staff in the Victorian Age shared their employer's status. The higher the status of those you served, the more elevated your position in society. Or so the butler kept telling her.

Ignoring Cuthbert's renewed interest, she tucked the binder back inside her bag, then turned to examine the grand portico. Jutting from the front of the manor, three arches made a home amid gothic architecture, creating a protected cove. She made some quick calculations. Wide, long, and deep. Lots of room. Enough to park eight or nine cars bumper to bumper, or three large carriages pulled by teams of four horses. She twisted in her seat, looking out the back window as Hendrix drove beneath the structure.

The vaulted ceiling and attention to detail set her imagination on fire, as did the frieze tucked in the corners, stretching from column to column. Her mouth curved. Trolls—a whole army of ugly carved in stone, each making a grotesque face from his lofty perch above her head.

Cuthbert sighed in disapproval.

She smiled. "So far, so good."

The driver's door opened and closed.

Ferguson slung her bag over her shoulder, then pulled on the door latch and pushed it open. Helped along by Hendrix, the heavy panel swung wide.

Slithering backward, he gave her the space she needed to exit. "If you'll follow me, my liege, I will show you to your—"

Hinges hissed. The double doors fronting The White Hare banged open.

A giant rodent dressed in a blue blazer thundered over the threshold. "Hendrix! Thank the stars, you've returned!"

Her mouth fell open.

With a flick of his scaly tail, Hendrix turned to face

the rodent-slash... Well, she didn't know what it was exactly. Not a rat or mouse, more like—

"Terrible news, I tell you!" Wringing his paws, the man-sized rodent hopped across the cobblestones. His velvet suit jacket bunched up. The burgundy tie he wore flew over his shoulder as his tufted ears twitched, swiveling forward only to fold back flat against the side of his head. "Terrible...terrible...*terrible!*"

"What is it, Ascot?" Hendrix asked, calm in the face of his employee's panic.

"Oh, sir, you're never going to believe it."

Hendrix raised a brow.

Ascot's whiskers quivered. "There's a dragon in the parlor."

"Which one?"

"The innkeeper's private study." Beady brown eyes turned in Ferguson's direction. "I'm so sorry, my l—"

"Liege," Hendrix said, interrupting Ascot before he broke her rule.

"Err, liege," Ascot said. "I tried to keep him out. Truly, I did, but you know dragons. They're impossible...impossible, impossible, *impossible!*"

The panicked screech echoed under the portico. As the wind carried it away, Hendrix glanced at her.

"I'll handle it," she said, stepping into the breech without knowing why.

Chalk it up to the alarm she saw in Hendrix's eyes, or maybe the fact she disliked that a dragon was frightening her staff. The reason didn't matter. Neither did the look of horror on the Hendrix's face. She needed to prove to herself, and everyone else, that Mavis knew what she was doing. By choosing Ferguson as heir, her godmother had signaled her intent, believing she could manage the inn.

Which meant she needed to start doing it. Right

off the bat. No way would she fold at the first sign of trouble. She'd quit her job, gotten on a plane of her own free will, and left a country she loved for one she no longer knew. No time like the present to put her stamp on the place.

"My liege, I think perhaps—"

"Do me a favor, would you, Hendrix?"

He swallowed. "Of course."

"Lead the way."

"You've only just arrived."

"I don't care," she said, gesturing toward the towering front doors. "There's a dragon in the parlor, Hendrix, and that simply will not do."

His lips curved.

She nodded back and, waving him ahead of her, followed him beneath the watchful eye of frowning trolls to the front entrance. He slithered. She walked, gaze roaming the pictographs craved into the face of the wooden doors. Hendrix opened one for her. She sailed through, shoulders square, only one thing on her mind. It didn't matter that she had no idea what she was doing. She must earn her staff's respect by taking the reins and solving the problem. Now, not later, after she settled in.

So...

Only one thing left for her to do—figure out how to kick the effing dragon out of the parlor so she could settle into her new home.

4

The spacious suite smelled of new paint...and powerful magic.

Dragging his fingertip along the antique table doubling as a desk, Kruger allowed his gaze to roam. The rambling flat with rooms that opened one into another didn't really qualify as a *suite*. More like a three-thousand-square-foot home kitted out with the best money could buy.

A male who enjoyed creature comforts, he appreciated the attention to detail: not crowded with furniture, fourteen-foot ceilings, ornate moldings, dark, wide-planked wooden floors, an army of windows that celebrated light, bright and airy. A recently designed space, no doubt with the new innkeeper's personal taste in mind.

Not that she'd be at The White Hare long. Less than twenty-four hours, if he got his way.

Mavis might've been a pain in the arse, but that didn't mean her replacement needed to become one. He had a plan. A good one that didn't include subtlety.

He wanted her off balance the second she stepped inside her new home. Mavis had warned him with her note: the heir apparent wouldn't be a pushover. In his experience, females rarely were, which meant he must attack before she managed to raise her guard. She needed to understand the magic surrounding the Parkland wouldn't stop him. He was a dragon warrior, one who could get to her anytime, anyplace.

Wandering out of her study, he paused between a set of black, steel-framed French doors. A long, low-slung couch stood opposite him. Navy-blue velvet with thick cushions. Two wide-bodied, rust-colored lounge chairs flanked it in front of a mantlepiece that, if he had to guess, was over a hundred years old.

Perfection everywhere he looked. Nothing out of place in a living room with paneled floor-to-ceiling walls painted a fresh, creamy white. A space that leaned toward feminine, but in which he felt comfortable, totally at home.

An odd thing for him to think.

Boots planted besides a wall of built-in bookcases, Kruger frowned at the colorful area rug, wondering about the female who planned to call the flat home. Foolish thoughts, a complete waste of his time. He knew it, and yet, curiosity kept speculation alive, making him wonder about a lot of things since his last visit to The White Hare. So many questions, too few answers. The one bothering him most, though, was: could he go through with it? Or was he doomed to fail?

The more Kruger examined the plan, the less he liked it. He was ruthless by nature, without mercy when going after what he wanted. A fact his brothers-in-arms enjoyed about him, and yet, right now, standing inside The White Hare, he hesitated to put his plan into play. He'd never frightened a female on purpose before—or contemplated killing one, either.

Flexing his fingers, Kruger glared at the chaise

longue sitting in front of windows set in a circular alcove. More blue velvet. Annoying as all fucking hell. If only he'd been made in the image of his sire—remorseless, with a heavy lean toward duplicity. If only he didn't feel—

Static clawed across his temples.

A link into mind-speak flared, allowing a deep voice to roll into his head. *"Target inbound."*

"How close?"

"Inside the lobby."

"What's she look like?"

Rannock chuckled. *"Yer about tae find out."*

"Ran—"

"Donnae ruin my fun, Ruger."

"Fuck." The loose hold Kruger had on his temper slipping. Why? No bloody idea. Rannock lived to give him shite. The feeling was mutual, bordering on pathological most nights as he and his packmate attempted to one-up each other. Tonight, though, he could've done without the usual aggravation. *"I'm kicking yer arse when we get home."*

"If you decide tae come home, then I'm game."

Kruger frowned. *"What the fuck's that supposed tae mean?"*

"Brace, brother."

Clenching his teeth, Kruger flicked at a throw pillow. The thing went flying, tumbling the length of her couch as he stepped off the area rug. Ancient floorboards creaked. Heavy footfalls echoed against high ceilings. The door latch clicked. Hinges murmured a second before the scent of gorgon drifted into the room.

Gaze riveted to the mouth of the hall, Kruger crossed his arms and waited. A wave of violence shimmered around the corner. An instant later, Hendrix came in. Shimmering yellow eyes narrowed on him. Hands curling into twin fists, the male bared his teeth.

A blatant show of disrespect. The gorgon knew better, was tempting fate... and doing it on purpose.

Kruger snarled, the lethal sound coming from deep inside his chest.

Hendrix's shoulder-length dreadlocks twitched. The weave of dark strands thickened at the tips, threatening to grow into serpent heads. "You are not welcome here."

"Like I give a shite." His attention strayed to the space beyond Hendrix. "I warned you, gorgon. I told you what would happen if—"

"Don't you dare."

Soft voice. Firm tone. An accent with lyrical notes Kruger couldn't place, but made him vibrate like a tuning fork.

"I've been traveling for twenty hours straight. I'm tired. I'm hungry. I'm an inch away from annihilating everyone in my path, so cut the effing crap. I'm not in the mood for your threats, or anyone else's."

The owner of the voice came around the corner.

He lost his ability to breathe.

Hearing his reaction, Rannock laughed.

Unable to look away, Kruger stared at her. She glared back, making his mind spin. Struggling to keep up, he shook his head. Whatever he expected, it hadn't been her. Nobody like *her*.

Fuck.

She was power at full speed. A high-energy female with an aura the color of Christmas—bright greens, fiery reds touched by hints of gold. Long hair the color of sunset piled in a messy bun on top of her head. Light green eyes so pale, the irises looked colorless. Freckles sprinkled across the bridge of her nose. Tall. Curvy. Carrying more weight than modern society dictated a female should, but on her? Perfection. Sheer beauty that worked in amazing ways.

Everything about her *worked*, making him yearn to get closer.

"Forgive me, my liege," Hendrix murmured, keeping his eyes on him but talking to the innkeeper. "If you're hungry, I can—"

"Chocolate. Anything with chocolate in it."

"A fresh croissant? Some coffee with chocolate syrup, perhaps?"

"That'd be great. Thanks, Hendrix." Thick binder pressed to her chest, she shifted behind the gorgon.

Her scent drifted into Kruger's air space.

Desperate for any part of her, he breathed deep. Evergreens and candy canes spiked with a hint of female musk. Delicious. Tempting. Maddening as primal need avalanched into full-blown arousal. Already taut muscles knotted as his dragon rose, begging to be let out of its cage—to touch and taste, to experience the fullness of her.

A catastrophe in the making.

He wasn't like other Dragonkind warriors. His bloodline ensured it. His sire was Silfer, the dragon god—a full-blooded beast, not a drop of human in the male. And his mother—half wood nymph, half human, which made Kruger one-quarter shy of a fully balanced load.

The unusual mix made him more aggressive than the rest of his kind. More powerful, too, able to shift between Dragonkind subsets, causing others to miscategorize him. The usual Dragonkind principles didn't apply to him. Some nights, his brothers-in-arms called him a venomous dragon. Other times, he got labeled an earth dragon, or even a Metallic depending on his mood.

Truth was, he didn't know where he fell on the continuum. He straddled the supernatural sphere, moving between skill sets when it served him, commanding more than one kind of magic. A gift from his bastard sire, no doubt.

Not that Kruger cared. The male hadn't loved him enough to fight for the right to raise him. Hell, could be his sire didn't love him at all. All evidence pointed in that direction. Silfer had discarded his mother the second she became pregnant and ignored Kruger after he was born, shirking his responsibilities, exiling his son to the Scottish Highlands.

Out of sight, out of mind. No love lost. Ever the way of gods and goddesses.

He tried not to think about it, tried not to wonder how different his life would be—how much more he'd understand about himself—if his sire had loved him. More useless thoughts accompanied by questions he needed to stop asking. He kept telling himself to put the past to bed, let his history go and accept the sharp edges of his nature. Some things, after all, couldn't be changed...and should never be lamented.

He wasn't built for deep connection. The interactions he had with his brothers-in-arms every night proved it. He stood on the fringes, a member of the Scottish pack while remaining an outsider. Unlike his packmates, Kruger didn't want a female of his own. He understood loyalty, not love. He enjoyed sex, not intimacy. A wealth of experience told him he wasn't capable of loving anyone. Fact not fiction, a simple statement of the truth, but—

Bloody hell. *Look at her.*

Glorious coloring. Gorgeous energy wrapped up in

a pretty package he wanted to explore. Having her under him, over him...shite. He didn't care how it happened, just as long as she landed in his bed, and he learned what she sounded like when she came. What she looked like when she—

"Who are you?"

Her voice hit him again. Prickles rampaged down his spine. Swallowing hard, Kruger tried to find his voice.

Hendrix beat him to it. "His name is Kruger, my liege."

Arching a bright copper brow, she threw the gorgon a sidelong glance. "I thought you said he was a dragon."

"He is, my liege. A dragon warrior from the Scottish pack."

"But..." She trailed off, sounding confused.

"Bloody hell," Kruger rasped, accidentally broadcasting his alarm through mind-speak.

A mistake. A big one Rannock wasted no time exploiting.

"Feel like flying home now?"

"Bugger off."

"Didnae think so," his friend said, unable to resist rubbing it in.

"Go home, Ran."

"No way." The heavy thump of wings beat through the line. *"Didnae get a close look at her earlier. I'm coming in. Gonna make sure it's all good, call the lads, fill 'em in, then—"*

"Do that, and I'll rip yer face off."

Rannock laughed.

Kruger drew a much-needed breath. His sonar vibrated. His heartbeat raged as territorial instinct carved out his insides. Pale eyes fixed on him, the innkeeper sidestepped Hendrix. The major-domo murmured a warning and blocked her by holding out his arm, preventing her from getting any closer.

Good call. The best, given Kruger's control lay in tatters.

He fought to contain his reaction. A noble battle, one Kruger knew he needed to win, but...

Goddess, with his beast rampaging, the urge to touch her bombarded him. Locking his frame, he withstood the barrage, but if she took one more step... just one fucking more...he'd snap, and she of the gorgeous energy and flaming red hair would end up naked beneath him.

Bad mojo. Terrible decision making.

He needed her scared shitless. He needed her gone. He needed to stick to the plan and complete the mission. Nothing but disaster would come from becoming attached to the innkeeper.

But as he held her gaze, ferocious need grabbed hold, spinning him in dangerous directions as logic died and desire took on a life of its own.

5

Blocked from moving into the living room, Ferguson didn't know what she wanted to do more—continue staring at Kruger, or call Hendrix crazy. The guy standing in her new apartment didn't look like a dragon. She'd expected scales, claws, sharp teeth, and bad breath. Or at the very least, to find him hoarding expensive silverware in the kitchen, but...

He looked human. Raw, elemental, fierce, for sure, but also all man.

Peering around Hendrix, she ran her gaze over Kruger again. Tall guy, built strong with wavy dark hair and beautiful bone structure. Physical perfection blunted by the sharp edge of intensity. The kind of man who commanded attention. A lot of it, no doubt making women everywhere stop short and stand up straighter. In the hopes of drawing his eye—for an hour, an afternoon, or, if she got lucky, an entire weekend.

Much like her ex-husband. A lot like her stepbrothers.

The world loved handsome men, laying bounty on silver platters at their feet. Easy pickings. Few hardships. Tons of entitlement shaped by the belief life owed them the best, and everyone in their orbit better fall in line.

The reminder jabbed at her. Anger flicked its thorny tail, nudging her temper.

An unfair reaction, maybe. One full of judgment. Something Kruger hadn't yet earned. She didn't know the guy, after all. Could be he wasn't anything like the men she'd left behind in Chicago. Could be nothing more than bad timing and frustration on his part. Could be a lot of things, but as she held his gaze, intuition gave her insight. Past experiences and still-open wounds did the rest. The fact the dragon warrior stood in her living room uninvited, acting like a jerk, signaled his intent.

Kruger wasn't the welcome wagon. He wanted something. Or worse, planned to upend her apple cart before she took control of The White Hare, making it impossible for her to settle into her new home.

Hugging the binder to her chest, she scowled at him.

Kruger flinched. Not a lot. Hardly at all before his expression went blank. His eyes, though, didn't lie. She caught the glimmer of unease, saw disquiet surface in the shimmering red band that ringed the outside of his pitch-black irises. The sharpening of his features gave him away too. His growl, though, landed like a blow. The low sound scrambled her composure, slipping beneath the surface of her skin.

Dormant parts of her woke in the sudden rush. Things she'd thought long dead. Errant urges her ex-husband helped kill. Heat and awareness. Vulnerability infused with a sense of purpose. The undeniable rise of femininity as appreciation crested and desire rolled. None of which she needed, given Kruger's ram-

pant masculinity more than matched the needs she'd
been denying.

She hadn't had sex in...

God, years. It felt like years. Could be years, given
the state of her marriage before she left.

Unbeknownst to her, Brent had continued playing
the field after the wedding: business meetings, client
events, weekends away to consult on cases. Great excuses. All of which she bought. No reason to doubt
him...at first. Three years in, after waking up alone—
again—she'd rolled out of bed with a knot in the pit of
her stomach, unable to put her finger on why, or understand the reason he no longer wanted her.

Six months after that, she confronted him, and
learned the ugly truth, reaping the disastrous results
of her inattention.

Guilt for her part in the fiasco rose.

Grabbing hurt by the tail, Ferguson wrestled it into
submission. Practice helped her stuff it back in its box
and slam the lid closed. Showing weakness wasn't a
good idea. Not right now. She needed to keep her head
in the game. Kruger was watching, looking for a soft
spot, wondering how best to push her over the edge.

Speculation? Outright paranoia? Maybe, but she
didn't think so.

Intuition warned her to be careful. The beautiful
man standing ten feet away might look human, but as
she studied him, his *otherness* became apparent. In the
same way she had with Montague, Ferguson sensed
the beast in him. Powerful. Hungry. Seething just beneath his surface. Like most predators, Kruger possessed sharp edges and unerring instincts. If she gave
him an inch, he'd steal a mile, leaving her to play
catch-up right out of the gate.

So...what to do? How best to handle him?

Strategizing in silence, Ferguson flipped through her options. She needed to go on the attack, keep him off balance, never allow him to find his footing or—

"Yer name?" he asked, eyes narrowed on her.

His brogue washed over her. Resonant timbre. Pitch perfect with gorgeous undertones. Pleasure chased a shiver down her spine. She murdered her reaction, killing the shimmy mid-quiver. He didn't need to know she found him attractive...or that the sound of his voice made her tingle in interesting places.

"Ferguson McGilvery," she said, struggling to maintain control.

"'Tis a male's name."

She looked down at her chest. Yup. Still there. A full D cup strapped into a sports bra, hidden behind the binder pressed to her chest. "Really?"

A muscle flexed in his jaw. "So, you're one of those."

"One of what?"

"A smart-ass."

"Could be," she said, stepping out from behind Hendrix.

The gorgon shook his head, warning her to stay behind him.

Patting his arm, she walked around Hendrix. She stopped five feet from Kruger, sending a clear message. She wasn't afraid of him and refused to be intimidated. Ferguson waited until understanding dawned in his eyes. The second it did, her attention left him, and she looked around. Unlike her tiny apartment in Chicago, her new place was bright and airy, stylish, with a lot of old-world charm. Not that she'd seen much, but if the rest of the place was anything like the living room, she wouldn't complain.

Her attention strayed to the wall of floor-to-ceiling bookcases. The tight tangle in her chest unraveled as she looked over the spines. A curated collection, one that would keep her in books for months. Thank God. A distraction. A place to unwind when the outside world got too loud and she needed peace and quiet.

"Anyone ever call you Fergie?"

Dragging her gaze from the books, she glanced at Kruger. "Close friends do, but since you aren't one of those, don't call me that."

"What should I call you, then?"

"Ms. McGilvery."

"You're shitting me."

She bit down on a smile. "Only fair, since you're here to piss me off."

"How do you figure?"

"You're succeeding, by the way," she said, ignoring his question. "Just in case you were wondering."

"Jesus," Kruger muttered. "Been here two minutes 'n' you're already a pain in the arse."

"You invaded my home. What did you expect in return—compliance?"

Annoyance flamed in his black eyes. A flicker of fire followed, licking over the tops of his shoulders. Curious thing, though—his t-shirt remained intact. No scorch marks on white cotton. Zero damage done to his skin as tendrils danced around the tattoo inked around one of his biceps.

She looked a little closer. Precise lines drawn by a steady hand. A black and gray design with scales half covered by the sleeve of his shirt. A snake, maybe? Could be a dragon too, but—

Hendrix cleared his throat. "Ah, my liege?"

"Uh-huh," she murmured, mesmerized by the fire dancing across Kruger's arm: crimson and emerald flames touched by gold, an interesting color combination. Kind of festive, actually.

"Perhaps it would be best to invite him to join you in a more public—"

Kruger snarled, exposing the sharp points of his canines.

"I'll take that snack now, Hendrix," she said without looking away from the dragon warrior about to lose his cool in her living room. "Though forget about the coffee. I'm gonna need a stiff drink instead."

Hendrix threw her a wild look. "I cannot leave you alone with him."

"He's not going to hurt me. We'll be fine." A calculated risk. A serious gamble that might cost her in the end, but some things couldn't be avoided. Kruger meant business. She needed to know why. "Won't we, Kruger?"

The shimmering glint in his eyes intensified.

Gaze boring into his, she raised a brow.

Kruger tipped his chin.

"You cannot trust him, my liege."

"I'm aware," she said, giving the gorgon a pointed look. One that stated she could not only handle herself, but knew what she was doing.

Guys like Kruger never responded to weakness. Given an opening, they crushed people, rolling over any and all objections, so no sense pussyfooting around.

"See you in a few, Hendrix."

"I'll be in the kitchen, my liege." Giving Kruger a perturbed look, the gorgon turned with a flick of his tail. Scales rasped over the floor as he disappeared through the French doors. "Not far away, if you have need of me."

"Got any tequila around?" she asked, tossing the

binder by Kruger. The corner grazed his arm before the binder landed in one of the armchairs. He frowned at her. A throw pillow hit the floor, then rolled into the glass-topped coffee table. "I could use a shot...or five."

Kruger watched the pillow a second, then glanced at her. "Spirits are in the study."

Spirits?

Ferguson froze. What did he mean? Had he seen something he shouldn't have? Was he able to see what she saw? The idea Kruger might be able to sense her ability—in the same way she read the complexities in his—rattled her.

No one else knew about her visitors. No one in the living world, at least.

Panic spiraled into full-blown paranoia, asking dangerous questions. Ignoring every single one, she kept her expression blank, then killed her reaction, resisting the urge to look over her shoulder. For Cuthbert, or Luther, or, heaven forbid, Jethro to appear in a puff of pot-infused smoke.

Kruger's brows snapped together. "Lass?"

The wariness in his voice nudged her. She raised a brow, going on the offense to cover her unease. "Spirits?"

"Aye."

Her stomach knotted. "What kind?"

"No clue. Wasn't here tae tie one on, so I didnae bother checking. Just saw a bunch of bottles in the sideboard."

"You've been snooping?"

Kruger shrugged.

"Know thine enemy?"

"Something like that."

Reassured he hadn't uncovered her secret, she

launched evasive maneuvers and pointed at the flames undulating on his skin. "You might want to put that out. Carbon monoxide, you know. Not good for anybody."

He glared at her, then grumbled something under his breath. The fire went out, infusing the air with cedar as tendrils of smoke rolled off his shoulders.

"You really should do something about that."

"What?"

"Yoga, maybe."

He scowled at her.

Ignoring the show of temper, she continued, "I hear meditation works wonders. Might help you unwind before whatever's got you tied in knots causes you to explode."

"I'm not—"

"Try again." She shrugged out of her peacoat and tossed the heavy wool jacket on the back of a chair. Quick strides took her past him, toward the entrance to the study. "You're wound tighter than an Oklahoma twister."

"A what?"

"Never mind. You wanted to talk. I'm giving you an opening. I shouldn't, given your blatant intimidation tactics, but I am, so—start talking."

"Fuck," he grumbled. "You're worse than she was."

"Who?"

"Mavis."

"You know my godmother?"

"Unfortunately."

"So what—you didn't get what you wanted from her, so now you're here to bully me?"

"I'm not bullying you."

"No?"

A muscle twitched in his jaw.

She clenched her teeth to keep from laughing. God. He was too easy. A much softer touch than expected, given the lethal vibes he wore like cologne. "Showing up uninvited. Breaking into my place. Snooping through my stuff. Acting like a badass, harassing my staff, trying to scare me. Seems—"

"If only it were working."

"—like intimidation to me."

He sighed.

She paused on the threshold to look over her shoulder. "You want me to go on?"

"Is the list extensive?"

She pursed her lips. "You haven't been here long enough for the list to be extensive, but given how annoying I find you so far, I'm sure we'll get there."

"Jesus, McGilvery. You always this difficult?"

"Depends."

"On what?"

"Whom you ask, and whether or not I like you."

"You got a male?"

The unexpected jab made her flinch. A mistake. The wrong one to make in the verbal chess match she'd started with Kruger.

A skilled strategist, Ferguson knew how to play the game. She'd been taught by the best, forced to learn on the fly. One moment insulated by love, the next set adrift when her mother never came home. She'd been eleven, and her stepbrothers fourteen. Even as teenagers, the pair knew how to hurt her. They never pulled their punches, aiming to hurt, maim, and, sometimes, destroy.

Her relationship with the boys hadn't been great before the accident. It got worse after her mother's death, and her stepfather checked out, refusing to intervene. He egged his sons on, or simply ignored the byplay. Which left her alone in a house full of guys who used nasty words, all-too-accurate putdowns and cruel pranks to keep her in line.

So she understood the game. When to dodge. When to parry. When to avoid and the best times to turn and fight. Which also made her able to read an opponent and know when one was about to seize the upper hand.

An advantage she handed Kruger by reacting. By giving away the truth.

"Of course you donnae have a male," he said, sensing her weakness, moving in for the kill. "What happened—you play the shrew and scare him away? Or mayhap he simply didnae want you anymore. Did he find someone else? That it, McGilvery? Is he at home, in the Americas, fucking someone else? Someone sweeter. Someone prettier, leaving you tae—"

"Shut up."

"Touchy."

"And you're an asshole."

"At least I'm getting laid."

The barb struck like an arrow, hitting the very heart of her. Just another nasty insult, one of many she'd fielded in recent years. A verbal strike designed to obliterate her self-esteem. A tried and true method, the ultimate weapon in a man's arsenal.

She swallowed past the tight knot in her throat as memories came flooding back. Old wounds reopened. Choking on the pain, Ferguson struggled to rally, but recovery, along with relief, remained out of reach.

Turning her back on him, she walked into the study, around the desk to the sideboard. Shaky hands unearthed two glasses and a bottle of scotch. Her second choice. Tequila would've gone down smoother, but the walking wounded took what they could get.

A quick scan told her she'd be drinking without ice.

After cracking the seal on the bottle, she poured without comment. Amber liquid hit the bottom of fine crystal. Prisms of color danced across the top of the antique sideboard. The scent of hard alcohol assaulted her senses. Silence did the rest, cranking her tight as heavy footfalls followed her into the room.

Kruger stopped on the other side of the desk.

Determined to keep the hurt from resurfacing, Ferguson took a sip. The mouthful burned all the way down. The second the scotch hit her stomach, though, warmth spread, allowing her to turn and face him.

His dark gaze met hers, then traveled over her face. Braced for another round of nastiness, she drew a fortifying breath, picked up the second glass, and reentered the game.

Feet planted beside the office chair, she reached across the desktop and offered Kruger the scotch. His expression softened. He accepted the drink. "Listen, McGilvery..."

"Say what you came here to say, then go."

"I didnae mean... I shouldnae—"

"Say it and go," she said, voice quiet, heart still stinging from the gut punch he'd landed.

A stupid reaction. Hurt feelings always landed a girl in trouble, twisting a situation until she couldn't see straight. No matter how nasty things got, Ferguson knew better than to take his comments personally. Kruger was no different than anyone else. He played the game to win, using the weapons at his disposal.

Something about him, though—his beauty, maybe...the idea a man like him would never desire a woman like her, a girl with carrot-orange hair who carried extra weight—cut deep, leaving new wounds in need of immediate attention.

Frowning at his glass, he drew in a deep breath. Something surfaced in his dark eyes. Something she didn't recognize. Remorse, maybe. A renewed sense of fair play, perhaps. Ferguson didn't care. He'd delivered the blow, skewering her without hesitation. Now he could effing well pay the price.

He cleared his throat. "I came tae make you an offer."

"What kind?"

"I want tae buy The White Hare."

"It's not for sale."

"Lass—"

"It's not for sale." Drilling down, she found her courage, met and held his gaze. "Nor will it ever be. I may have just arrived, but I already know that much."

"You've yet tae see what I'm offering."

"I don't need to."

And she didn't. Not now, not ever.

She'd felt the connection the moment Hendrix turned up the lane and the hotel reached out to greet her. To welcome her. To draw her into the fold.

The spark burned in her veins, growing stronger by the minute. As it flared bright, realization dawned: she belonged here. Destiny awaited her here, making her feel things she hadn't since her mother died—acceptance and unconditional love. The spirit of The White Hare wanted her right where she stood, inside the Parkland. So did her godmother. Mavis needed her to stand strong and ensure the legacy of her line not only lived on, but thrived.

A lot rested on the success of The White Hare.

She'd read the treatise explaining the Parkland's

role—along with *Udo's Guide to Magical Creatures*—on the trip over. The hotel she now owned was a refuge, one of the last of its kind, a rare respite in a violent world for all manner of Magickind, free of the on-going feuds between different species. Some hunted others for sport. Most fought over territory and dwindling resources. A couple of wars had lasted centuries, which made places like The White Hare all the more important.

The hotel welcomed all kinds—vampires, werewolves, gargoyles, druids and demigods, all manner of shifters, nymphs, sprites, and fairies—providing a safe haven and clear guidelines for those who stayed under its roof.

So...no. She wouldn't be selling her birthright. Or betraying the long line of innkeepers who'd come before her.

"Fergie," he murmured, ignoring her wishes by using her nickname. "You've no idea what you've gotten into here."

"And what—you know better?"

"I'm part of this world. I belong in it."

"So do I."

"Not in the same way I do."

An icy breeze drifted into the room, raising goosebumps on her arms, heralding an arrival.

Cradling his black cat in his arms, Cuthbert appeared in the doorway. Little more than a hazy outline, the butler frowned at Kruger. Luther meowed, which she took as a sign of support.

Hold the line.

Draw a hard, hard line.

As the words whispered through her mind, she leveled her gaze on Kruger. "Feel free to find your way to the door."

Planting his palm on the edge of her desk, he leaned toward her. "You need tae know, you're never going tae win. Not against me."

Her hand tightened around her glass.

Murder in his eyes, Cuthbert stroked Luther's fur and looked around. Gliding toward a bookshelf, he examined a collection of paperweights, no doubt trying to decide which one would work best to crush Kruger's skull.

Ferguson shook her head slightly, warning the butler to stay put. She didn't want him throwing anything, never mind maiming the dragon warrior who'd invaded her space. Kruger would lose his temper. Bad things would follow. Things instinct warned her she might not survive.

"I'm looking out for you, lass."

"Yeah, right."

"I am," Kruger said, sounding sincere.

"No, you just want what you want, and don't care how you get it. But you need to get this, Kruger. Really look at me. Unlike Mavis, I'm not seventy-three years old. I'm not someone heading into my golden years, someone you can wear down and bully." Rotating her glass, she watched expensive scotch slosh against cut crystal. "Nothing you say—nothing you do—will change my mind."

"Stubborn," he said, glowering at her. "So bloody stubborn."

"Must run in the family, since Mavis refused to sell to you too."

He opened his mouth, no doubt to say something nasty about her godmother.

"Be careful," she said, itching to reach out and slap him. Prudence stayed her hand. "Very, very careful."

Irritation flashed in his eyes. He slammed his glass

down on her desk. Scotch flew over the lip onto his hand. He flicked his fingers.

Cuthbert gasped in outrage as liquid splattered across the leather blotter.

Unaware he had an audience, Kruger snarled a command. Papers appeared in his hand. With a snap of his wrist, he slapped the bundle down in front of her. Lots of legal mumbo-jumbo on the first page. "Read that. You've got three days. I'll be back after that tae discuss terms."

"Don't."

"What?"

"Bother coming back." Calm in the face of his ferocity, she took another sip. "Hendrix is right...you're not welcome here."

He pointed to the contract. "Read it. Consult a solicitor, hire one, I donnae give a shite...just *read it* and be ready tae sign."

Ready to sign? Was he out of his mind?

Her eyes narrowed. She leaned toward him. "What are you—deaf? Or simply too spoiled to take no for an answer?"

"Donnae test me, *fazleima*."

"Don't threaten me, dragon."

"Good for you, Ferguson," Cuthbert murmured.

With a low snarl, Kruger slammed the side of his fist against the papers, then turned on his heel. Throwing her another irate glance, he stormed out of the room, mumbling to himself, "Why did I even bother? Shoulda done what I wanted tae from the beginning. Fireball, meet car. Problem solved. Now I've gotta deal with another fucking innkeeper, a redhead and her..."

His voice trailed off, getting trampled beneath the loud thud of his boots across wooden floorboards. A moment later, a door slammed, rattling window panes, including the ones behind her.

Ferguson stared unseeing at the spot she'd last seen him, then downed her scotch in one go. Grabbing the bottle by the throat, she poured another. *Fireball, meet car. Problem solved.* She slugged back another shot. Seriously? Was Kruger so entitled, so intent, such a bad loser, he'd go so far as to—

"Did he just threaten tae kill you?" Hendrix asked, slithering into the room.

Cuthbert hopped out of the way to avoid getting walked through. An unpleasant experience by all accounts.

"Meow," Luther said, complaining about the sudden movement.

"Is that going to be a problem?" she replied, eyeballing the gorgon carrying a plate piled high with croissants. She took a second to count the pastries. Ten total, some with chocolate dribbled on top, others without.

Her brows drew together. Did Hendrix really expect her to eat all of that?

She yanked the chair away from her desk. The adrenaline that helped her go toe to toe with Kruger leaked out of her system, allowing weariness to set in. With a sigh of relief, she sat down. "Do you think Kruger is capable of killing me?"

"Probably, though..."

"What?"

"As a rule, dragon warriors do not hurt females. Unlike other Magickind, their need tae protect is instinctual."

"Well," she said, raising her glass to salute Hendrix, "at least I have that going for me."

"He won't stop, my liege."

"I know."

"We need a plan."

Did they ever. One that might include calling in the military. Or a bunch of orcs from *The Lord of the Rings*.

"Do you know why he's so focused on The White Hare?"

Kruger's interest in the inn wasn't just business. His desire to own it surpassed mere acquisition. He might like a challenge, but she'd sensed his desperation. He'd vibrated with it, casting such a strong energy field she'd been able to read it. Whatever drove him was powerful and rooted in secrecy.

No way of knowing for sure. Complete speculation on her part, but as she replayed the encounter in her mind, intuition spoke to her. Kruger was hiding something. Something huge. A problem he believed could be solved by acquiring The White Hare.

Swiveling her chair toward the windows, she stared out into the darkness. "Hendrix?"

"Yes?"

"Did Mavis say anything to you about Kruger?"

"Very little, but then, she wasn't like you. She never provoked him."

"Why not?"

"He's a dragon warrior, my liege. Very unpredictable. I believe she felt it best tae keep him at a distance."

An interesting approach. One she might be able to deploy if she understood Mavis's tactics. "How'd she manage that?"

"With a shotgun."

In the middle of taking another sip, Ferguson snorted. She sputtered as scotch went down the wrong pipe. "God, I would've paid to see that. Did he run for cover when she aimed a load of buckshot at his ass?"

"He wasn't pleased, but it took him over a month to come back."

"Hmm."

"What are you thinking?"

"That I'm going to need the shotgun."

"Are you a good shot?"

"Not particularly."

A wicked gleam in his eyes, he set the plate down in front of her. "I have an old cricket bat somewhere around here. In the closet, perhaps."

"Good thinking." Setting the scotch aside, she plucked a pastry from the top of the pile.

"The more weaponry, the better," Cuthbert said.

Ferguson couldn't disagree.

Kruger wouldn't give up or be dissuaded easily. He'd be back in three days.

She needed to be ready. First step—dig up more intel about the dragon pack in the area. Second step—find out why Kruger refused to walk away. She knew he had his reasons, compelling ones. The trick now would be unearthing the truth as quickly as possible, before his frustration boiled over and idle threats turned into real ones.

6

Gifted with a dragon's-eye view, Grizgunn scanned the ground, searching for signs of trouble. A force of habit. An unnecessary one, given serious problems rarely crossed his path these days. Soon, though, he'd launch his offensive and all that would change.

He'd have nothing but trouble then.

A welcome change after months of preparation. He was ready, tired of the stalemate, sick of strategizing instead of attacking, eager to move past caution and enter the game.

Angling his wings, he swung east toward the coast. Moonlight illuminated the fog rolling along low stone walls and winding roads. His gaze tracked the ruins in the distance. Home sweet home. Ten minutes max and he'd be underground, jogging down the steps into his lair. A hop, skip, and jump away from the hot springs—a feature the warriors under his command hated, but he enjoyed more than any Dragonkind warrior should. A quirk of character he couldn't explain—and his best friend didn't understand. He wasn't a water dragon, but that didn't stop him from enjoying a good swim. Especially when it came with warm water and clean scales.

Another deviation in his nature. As a skull dragon who leaned toward venomous, he should love dirt and digging, along with the host of germs that came with it. The more bugs the better, except...

He couldn't stand filth. Didn't want to think about it, or have any smudged across his light blue scales. Just the thought made him sick to his stomach, which naturally led to lots of handwashing and habitual trips to the subterranean pool deep inside his new home.

Lining up his approach, Grizgunn swung south, then banked north. His night vision flickered, picking up trace energy as he adjusted his sonar, cranking the dial until blurry became pinpoint sharp. Gaze roaming a stretch of rough coastline, he widened the grid, expanding his search area.

Lots of rocky terrain interrupted by the brilliant flashes of green grass in open fields. A few animals foraging in the underbrush of dense patches of forest. No humans in sight. Nothing but stormy skies, damp air, and the thundering sound of waves.

The North Sea snarled. Whitecaps slammed into the base of the cliffs. A vicious downdraft buffeted him. The twin tips of his split tail whiplashed.

He bared his fangs, enjoying the rising tempest along with Mother Nature's attitude. Two minutes from touchdown, he rocketed over a graveyard. Centuries-old tombstones shook. The rattle-'n'-roll rippled into open air as he banked into a wide turn above the old abbey. Ahead of him, Hakon put on the brakes. His XO's black, red-tipped scales flashed against the night sky as he folded his wings. The male dropped like a stone, landing between two massive monoliths standing in a circle of many.

Sharp claws scraped over moss-covered stone. Static blew into his head.

Hakon's voice came over the line. *"Land, Griz."*

He really should. Sooner rather than later, before dawn arrived and deadly UV rays pierced early-morning fog. More sensitive than most of his kind, he never played chicken with the sun. A smart male understood his own limitations, but even as prudence urged him to land, Grizgunn whirled into another turn. He loved flying in heavy mists. Nothing felt better than the wet whisper of spring against his scales.

The North Sea lashed at him, crashing into the base of the crag, throwing spray three hundred feet in the air.

He grinned.

Hakon growled. *"Griz—stop screwing around."*

Attention on the male glaring at him from the ground, he circled into a holding pattern. An orange line appeared on the horizon. He flipped up and over, playing in the current. Contrails whistled off the hooked tips of his wings. A few more minutes. Five, maybe six more. Cloud cover would protect him a little longer, ensuring the day didn't dawn too brightly.

Tempting fate, he spiraled into another revolution. The smooth glide dragged his mind away from his to-do list. After hours spent taunting the Scottish pack, the quiet flight home always put him in a good mood. Every time he saw the crumbling cathedral from the air, he thought the same thing—*what a spectacular find.*

Off the beaten path, forgotten by the world, the sprawling ruin provided everything he needed—comfort, privacy, complete safety from a global community gone mad. No one but his pack made their way so far north. History buffs stayed away. Animals gave the place a wide berth. With the powerful shielding spell sparking—hiding his new home from human and Dragonkind alike—only creatures with a death wish would be stupid enough to approach the Danish lair.

Assessing the invisible monster surrounding his lair (one that took him almost a week to conjure), he dipped low, then flipped up and over. Nasty energy raked his scales. Grizgunn grinned. The spell was a thing of beauty: bitter, bad-tempered, vicious, even to those it protected.

Grizgunn loved its attitude.

His warriors didn't share his opinion, disliking the tantrums the spell threw every time one requested entrance into the underground complex beneath the ruins. He heard the cursing, was aware of all scrapes and bruises, but didn't care, brushing aside his packmates' complaints.

With the enemy actively searching for his stronghold, he needed the extra protection. Reprimanding the spell for being too rough wasn't productive. Neither was lessening the monster's magical load. He wanted it strong. He needed it nasty. Ever evolving. Always adapting. Completely loyal to him and the warriors he commanded.

The game of hunt and destroy he played with Cyprus (commander of the Scottish pack) was a dangerous one. Not for the faint of heart, or a male who didn't understand the risks and know how to mitigate them.

The Scottish pack's reputation was well established. The warriors he taunted were vicious, without mercy, and skilled. Dragonkind commanders all over the world shied away from tweaking Cyprus's tail. Grizgunn had chosen to do the opposite—engage instead of avoid. Provoke instead of fly away. Kill instead of choosing to just survive.

Most considered him crazy. His warriors had too... at first.

But he couldn't let it go, refused to let the insult inflicted by the Scottish pack on his family line fester.

Fifty years was a long time to wait to right a wrong, but no matter the time frame, a Dragonkind warrior never forgot. His sire certainly hadn't, training Grizgunn for war, making him vow to avenge him—and reclaim his birthright—before unleashing him on the world. If only his sire were alive to see how much progress he'd made, to experience each victory along with the fallout as his son wreaked havoc on the Scottish Highlands and the communities Cyprus protected.

The whoreson deserved it all. Every bit of Grizgunn's fury, along with the agony of knowing he failed to defend his territory from a warrior king far cleverer than him.

He hummed in satisfaction.

Cyprus the pretender. The arrogant male needed to be sliced open and left to die. The slower the commander of Scottish pack bled out, the better. Every last drop squeezed out until the male's heart stopped beating, and he turned to dragon ash and blew away on the wind.

Grizgunn's sire would've been proud of his efforts. Had he lived, he would've patted him on the back, extolled his son's virtues to anyone willing to listen, and—

"Commander!" Hakon barked from the ground. *"What are you doing—trying to get fried?"*

Grizgunn blinked as a sunburst exploded over the water. The bright wave flicked its lethal tail. Dark skies vanished as poisonous UV rays sliced through the clouds. Heat rippled over his scales. Pain burned across his shoulders, raking like blades down his spine.

Smoke rolled off the hard shell of his interlocking dragon skin.

With a curse, Grizgunn folded his wings. His paws slammed down on compacted earth. Momentum tossed him sideways. Gritting his teeth, his curled his claws into the turf. Chunks of stones pinged off the outer shell of the church. The scent of peat moss burst into the air, joining the smell of singed scales.

Already in human form, Hakon sprinted beneath a broken archway. Shifting out of dragon form, Grizgunn hauled ass behind him.

Sunlight crept over the top of crumbling walls. Raising his arm to shield his light-sensitive eyes from the glow, he stayed on his warrior's heels and snarled a command. Magic exploded up the center aisle. An effervescent shimmer slammed into the nave at the front of the church. The spell protecting the lair twitched, then turned, flicking the tips of its barbed whip.

Black eyes narrowed on him from inside the magical abyss. Hakon cursed. Grizgunn growled in warning.

The shield snarled back, but yielded without throwing the usual tantrum. Cold air heated as the portal began to open. Footfalls thumping, Grizgunn ran. Stone scraped against stone. The heavy slab topping the altarpiece slid sideways, revealing a narrow staircase that descended into the underground lair. Boot soles scrambling over cracked mosaic tiles, Hakon dove into the opening.

Grizgunn vaulted up the steps, onto the platform

fronting the nave. Throwing himself forward, he slid like a baseball player. The side of his leg rasped across flat stones engraved with the names of humans laid to rest beneath the cathedral floor. His foot caught the top step. Sunlight burned over the back of his neck. Blisters bubbled across his skin. Another curse. More scrambling, and he somersaulted down the stairs headfirst.

Hakon snarled.

The slab snapped shut, enclosing them in darkness.

Grizgunn's shoulder slammed into the side wall. *"Fuck."*

"You idiot," Hakon said from the landing at the bottom of the first flight. Gray eyes the color of smoke began to glow, painting a target on his chest. *"Swear to Silfer, Griz. Next time you pull that shit, I'm gonna—"*

"You think you got enough juice to take me?"

"After witnessing that shit, it'd be fun to try. Someone's gotta knock some sense into you."

Grizgunn sighed. Trust Hakon to give it to him straight. The male took honesty to extremes, getting in his face when no other warrior dared. A trait he appreciated about his friend, and the entire reason he'd appointed the male XO of the Danish pack. Which meant he needed to stop being an idiot and start giving Hakon his due.

"Sorry."

Hakon blinked. His gaze flickered like a dying flashlight. *"What did you just say?"*

"Don't give me any shit," Grizgunn said, dropping mind-speak as he touched the back of his neck. Singed skin, totally crispy, and enough pain to piss him off. "I've got a lot on my mind. Was rethinking our strategy up there and got distracted for a minute."

"Or ten."

Grizgunn clenched his teeth. "What'd I say about giving me shit?"

"You were circling up there like a fucking vulture. I know you can't wait to pick over the Scottish pack's bones, but...come on, Griz."

"Hakon—"

"You know what we're up against. I can't pull this off without you. We need to be on the same page, not fucking around with—"

"I know, *bror*," he murmured, calling his warrior "brother" in Danish, defaulting to his native tongue. A longstanding habit, something that settled him when stress crept in. "Hard to forget when it's all I ever think about."

Twisting his head to one side, Hakon cracked his neck. "You going to take the money?"

The ten-million-dollar question.

Literally.

That was how much money sat on the table. A candlelit one set by Rodin to seduce him into the fold...and under the Archguard's thumb.

"Haven't decided yet." He glanced up as the light globes above his head activated, throwing illumination in soft waves. "I'm not a fan of the conditions."

Hakon grunted. "Or the restrictions."

"Rodin's help comes with strings, Hakon. A lot of them."

"Maybe, but with it, we'd have been able to pay Montgomery, and the Scot would be caged in our dungeon right now."

Hakon wasn't wrong. A bone of contention between Grizgunn and his new XO...along with a missed opportunity. Having the upper hand while trying to kill Cyprus and the assholes he commanded would've been sweet. What amounted to icing on the proverbial cake, but draining his resources to get a hold of Vyroth (Cyprus's blood brother and identical twin) had seemed irresponsible. Like shooting himself in the foot instead of using his claws to rip apart the enemy.

He'd spent years saving for the war with the Scottish pack. Every penny he earned as a mercenary while exiled in Denmark got thrown into the fund, to aid the cause as he worked to undo the injustice done to his sire.

"Water under the bridge," he murmured, starting down the stairs toward his friend. "Can't go back, gotta move forward."

"Still pisses me off."

"I know, but..." Pausing on the landing, Grizgunn slapped his XO on the back. "The new warriors should help lighten the load. Got any good candidates?"

Hakon scowled. "Not as easy as it sounds."

"You're still in the process of screening?"

"Two dozen applicants so far, and still...nothing. But the next batch looks promising. Lots of firepower."

"Skill sets?"

"Got a water dragon on tap. He's got a couple of warriors with him who look—"

Grizgunn stopped short and pivoted to face Hakon on the stairs. "Water dragon?"

"Yah. Surprised the hell out of me he showed, but I'm glad he did. The male's a powerful motherfucker. Bad attitude, sharp skills, lethal instincts. A bit beat up. No idea what happened to him or why, but he could be a good addition to our pack if..."

"If?"

"We can control him."

A risk. A big one, if what Hakon said turned out to be true.

Water dragons were rare, little more than myths in Dragonkind circles. For centuries, his kind had believed males with smooth scales, webbed paws, and a love of water were nothing more than old wives' tales. Grizgunn had always known better. He'd seen one while hunting a Russian deserter in Norway. A complete accident. Even so, he'd gotten out of the warrior's territory fast, refusing to tweak that particular dragon's tail.

Frowning, Grizgunn rubbed his bruised shoulder. "I want to meet him."

"Figured."

"Set it up."

"I told him you'd be available tomorrow night."

"Where?"

"Edinburgh—back gardens, Holyroodhouse."

"The palace?"

"Why not?"

Enjoying his warrior's irreverence—and disdain of all things human—Grizgunn smiled. "On the grounds?"

"Lots of big trees there. Good cover. Landlocked. Far from the water. Better if the male tries something."

"Good," he murmured, chewing on the facts.

Only an hour's flight away. Not too close to the main Danish lair. Just far enough away to keep warriors from following him home. A necessary precaution, given none of the new recruits would share his space. A secondary lair was already under construction fifty miles south of Aberdeen. Any male smart enough to join the cause would be housed inside it, nowhere near the flashy digs Grizgunn shared with his personal guard.

"Could break in, have the meeting in one of the rooms," Hakon said when Grizgunn hesitated. His warrior knew him well, understanding how much he enjoyed breaking the toys humans liked to showcase... and brag about. Tourist destinations were a particular favorite of his. So much history. All those precious artifacts. So many expensive things to destroy. "Turn over some tables. Break some shit. Give the human authorities some ghosts to chase."

Grizgunn shook his head. No matter how much the idea of wrecking the palace interested him, he needed to be smart. Already behind schedule, he couldn't afford any more delays. His pack needed an infusion of new blood, warriors who not only knew how to fight, but held no love for the Scottish pack. Recruits had been surprisingly easy to come by. The applicants ranged from young to old, telling him more about Cyprus's methods than the whoreson wanted him to know.

The Scottish commander hadn't spent time making friends after he closed the island's borders. His enemies, however, seemed to be everywhere, answering the Danish pack's call, coming out of the woodwork after decades of being denied entrance into Scotland. Cyprus disliked interlopers. He chased stray males out of his territory on a regular basis, refusing to allow any to join his pack.

Which left the field of prime talent wide open.

He planned to tap into that error in judgment and seize what he needed—the upper hand in the war he'd started with the male who stole his crown along with the territory his sire had been destined to rule.

Reaching the bottom of the stairs, he murmured a command. Magic crackled. The seal around the door into the underground lair broke. Heavy duty hinges hissed as a door carved from solid granite swung inward. Thick stone grated against the uneven floor.

Grizgunn dipped his head beneath the low lintel, crossed the threshold, and—

"Finally," Tigmar said, twitching where he stood six feet away.

Halting just inside the entryway, Grizgunn drew a calming breath. He needed a second...along with the extra oxygen. Every time he saw Tigmar, he reacted the same way—with barely leashed violence. And even less tolerance.

Paranoid to the point of neurotic, Tigmar rubbed him the wrong way, making it difficult for Grizgunn to keep from punching him in the face. He'd dreamed about doing it, longed to wind up and shit-can the twitchy fucker so badly, he struggled to control the urge. He managed to, just barely, clinging to his resolve by a thread, containing his temper with the aim of keeping his computer geek alive.

Giving in to the satisfaction of splitting the male in two wouldn't get him what he needed—intel, the indispensable kind Tigmar pulled off the internet every time he cracked open a computer. If the information existed, the twitchy SOB wouldn't stop until he dug it up. Which meant Grizgunn couldn't kill him—no matter how much he wanted to most nights.

Sidestepping him, Hakon took the lead. A good call, given Grizgunn still fought the urge to beat the shit out of Tigmar.

Hakon tipped his chin. "Find something?"

"Kind of," Tigmar said, shifting from foot to foot. The open laptop he cradled quivered as he tried to stay still and failed.

Grizgunn's eyes narrowed. "Explain."

Tigmar cleared his throat. "Well, I've been poking around, hunting for sources of revenue—you know, shadow companies, shell corporations the Scottish pack might be using to hide financial transactions—and I stumbled onto something. An insulated umbrella company called KDH Capital. It's massive. Whoever owns it is a pro, moving companies around the board like chess pieces. Fortune 500 companies run by human CEOs and board members all over the world."

Interest sharpened his focus. Venomous mist swirled up his throat, polluting the air around him. "What does that mean?"

"I'm not sure what it means yet or even if—"

"Spit it out, Tigmar."

Hakon threw him a pointed look. The expression on his XO's face told him to cool it, to go gently instead of allowing annoyance to lead. The more impatient Grizgunn became, the twitchier Tigmar got, making him lose his train of thought along with his ability to talk.

With a sigh, Grizgunn powered down. No sense winding Tigmar up just to watch him go. "Tell me, *bror*. Whatever you've found, I'm sure it'll be helpful."

Hakon grunted in approval.

Pleasure replaced the worry in his computer geek's eyes. "The White Hare."

"What's that?"

Chewing on his bottom lip, Tigmar shrugged. "I can't find anything about it online. No website or mention of it anywhere, but by following the breadcrumbs, I found a shell company. That led to a few others, and when I dug deeper, I found a contract drawn up by a law firm owned by humans. Someone's trying to buy The White Hare, and if I'm right, given the pattern of financial data, it might be the Scottish pack."

"Let me see," Hakon murmured, moving around to look at the laptop screen.

"I printed it out." Vibrating like a tuning fork, Tigmar met his gaze, blue eyes full of hope, signaling he wanted nothing more than to please his leader. "I left everything on your desk, commander. I can walk you through all the transactions. Tell you why I think—"

"Good. Let's do that now, *ja*?"

"Sure thing, Grizgunn, sure. Anything you want."

Anything he wanted. Sounded exactly right. Especially if Tigmar gave him a hard target instead of the usual fluff. The second he identified the mark, Grizgunn would use what Cyprus wanted to acquire to draw the Scots out into the open, then tear the thieving whoresons apart.

7

Quiet drifted through the lair like spindles of eerie fog, lying in wait for his brothers-in-arms to roll out of bed and banish the silence. Acutely aware of the absence of sound, Kruger stepped out of the shower. Steam rolled out behind him, puffing against his bare back. He allowed the invasion of his space a moment, then murmured his wishes. The door swung closed, trapping the mist inside the glass enclosure as his magic went to work. Water droplets sizzled on his skin, then vaporized. Damp air cleared. Fog on the mirrors over the double vanity with marble countertops disappeared, reflecting crisp white tile with blue trim.

Listening hard, hoping to hear one of his pack-mates up and moving, he stepped off the bath mat and walked into his bedroom. A king-size bed stood to his left, mattress askew on the low platform, cotton sheets twisted, coverlet a heap on the floor. The tangle broadcasted his chaotic state of mind, stating plainly he hadn't slept—at all.

Not an optimal outcome.

Lack of sleep was a problem, worse for him than other Dragonkind warriors. Well rested he was a se-

rious threat to others. Tired with his emotions frayed
and thoughts tangled, he was a ticking time bomb.
One set to go off in a hurry if he didn't redirect his energy and quell the volatile nature of his need. He
needed a distraction. Something to shift his focus and
occupy his mind. If he stayed on his current course,
one of his packmates—or goddess forbid, one of their
females—would end up hurt.

Skirting the knotted mess on his bed, Kruger conjured a pair of basketball shorts, but nothing else. No
need for a shirt or shoes. His internal temperature ran
too hot to ever wear much. Sometimes he pushed the
boundaries of comfort and yanked on a t-shirt. His
mated packmates appreciated his efforts. Their females, however, didn't care, telling him to be himself,
never complaining about his preference for going
shirtless inside the lair.

The large vent above his head rattled. A stream of
icy air washed over him.

Tipping his head back, Kruger breathed it in, enjoying the chill as his internal temperature started to
rise. Inferno-like heat rolled across his nape. He
closed his eyes. Maybe another ice bath would help.
Maybe he needed Levin to conjure him another snowdrift to sit in. Maybe he should give the breathing ex-
ercises Wallaig taught him another try. Not that
anything his brothers-in-arms suggested ever worked.
His dragon was too unstable—or mayhap too sensitive
—to be contained when problems weighed heavy on
his mind and solutions remained thin on the ground.

His cross to bear. Part of his nature as he fought
the fire and lost.

Green and gold flames punched through his spine.
Embers sparked across his skin, making him unsafe
for mixed company. What he needed was a good fight,

a way to exorcise his demons and settle his mind. But
with Rannock still dead to the world—no doubt
wrapped around his mate, content to laze the day
away—Kruger's outlet had disappeared. Tempel might
be a good choice of sparring partner. Levin and Tydrin
too, but as he sent his senses searching, nothing came
back.

Everyone was still abed. All quiet on the Scottish
lair front. No one to punch. No one to piss off. No one
to help him contain the volatility—or the conflagra-
tion unfurling around his torso.

Toxic fumes spilled into the air. Stone walls
trembled.

Feet planted, fists clenched, Kruger bowed his
head and forced himself to focus. Little by little, the
fire moved from out of control to somewhat contained.
He pushed it from his belly, up his chest, around his
neck, then down his back. Flames caught hold between his shoulder blades, rolling up and down his
spine as he embraced the burn, allowing his dragon
the outlet, then opened his hands and flicked his
fingers.

The fireproof steel door opened without making a
sound.

Putting himself in gear, Kruger dipped his head
beneath the lintel and turned up the main corridor.
Bare soles whispering over dark hardwood, he walked
past an army of closed doors in a sea of pale granite.
Lots of claw marks on stone. A few scorch marks from
Wallaig's flamethrower exhale. Old scars delivered by
dragon claws rippling up to meet sixteen-foot ceilings.

All normal. Nothing out of place. Same old, same
old...except for the echo of nothingness driven by in-
activity.

Total silence. No relief in sight.

Kruger released a pent-up breath. The rasp echoed through the hush. He repeated the exercise, doing what Wallaig suggested, inhaling deep, exhaling smooth, trying to level out, but...fucking hell. Nothing he tried helped. The quiet only made things worse.

Especially after what had happened last night.

He needed a diversion. Right now. Before he made another mistake and even more of a mess.

With a low curse, he shook his head and kept his feet moving. The situation was more than just challenging. It was messed up. His reaction—along with his behavior inside The White Hare—crossed lines.

Not much raised his blood pressure. He couldn't think of a single thing that had pushed him over the edge in the last two centuries. Difficult negotiations— no problem. Hard-nosed strategies that deployed brutal tactics—acceptable. Troublesome CEOs and hostile takeovers—bring it on. Corporate battles enlivened him. Winning in the world of business was what he did...so, nay, he never lost sleep over exerting his will, wasn't prone to tossing and turning...until he met *her*.

Eighteen hours of hell. And it wasn't over yet.

Stepping off smooth hardwood planks onto a mishmash of soft rugs, he strode into the common room. Ignoring the colorful stained-glass dome above his head, he skirted a cluster of deep armchairs, then walked between the twenty-foot sectional and the mounted TV. He shook his head. The screen was massive, a recent addition that took up most of the wall. One that Tempel, the newest member of the Scottish pack, insisted he needed to watch his favorite teams. Something about the NFL, the Premier League, and Australian rules football. Not that Kruger gave a shite. Unlike the American male, he wasn't into sports.

Tempel kept trying to change his mind. Kruger continued to ignore him, preferring the ring—and sparring with Rannock—to sitting on his arse watching a bunch of humans dressed in ridiculous uniforms run around a field.

Bypassing the double swinging doors into the kitchen, he jogged up a set of stairs. Five steps up, and he entered the lair's nerve center. The computer hub where Ivy spent most of her time was to his left. The new library where Elise curated the pack's rare book collection took up all the space to his right. He glanced through the double glass doors as he walked past. No Elise, which meant no Cyprus.

Thank fuck.

Out of all the males he wanted to see right now, his commander wasn't one of them. The last thing he needed was to come face to face with Cyprus. The male wasn't stupid, far from it, which equaled disaster for Kruger right now. Unlike the other Scottish warriors, Cyprus possessed the ability to read him. One look and the male would know something was wrong. He'd demand an explanation, then poke and prod until Kruger gave him one.

Not advisable, given his current mood. And the fact he couldn't pinpoint the problem—or figure out what the hell was wrong with him.

Though he knew the source. The second he laid eyes on her, Kruger clocked the threat. Identifying the target wasn't the problem. His reaction to her, however? As serious as a being flambéed by a Dragonkind warrior who exhaled Scald.

He didn't understand it. Sure, Ferguson was pretty. He enjoyed looking at her, no question, but he met, charmed, and fucked beautiful females all the time.

He never wavered, got pulled off task...or wanted to take any of them home.

Halfway down the hall, he murmured a command. Magic flicked out in front of him. The electronic keypad lit up. He punched in the code with his mind, then watched the steel door depicting dragons in full flight swing wide.

Without breaking stride, he crossed the threshold. The scent of cedar and wood smoke curled against his senses. He breathed deep, allowing the cool recesses of the room to envelop him.

Reacting to his presence, twin desk lamps flipped on. Light poured across the steel-framed, glass-topped desk and modern office chair behind it. He loved the space he'd commandeered as his own. Everywhere he looked, old-world charm complemented modern décor. Slick gray couch with matching square backed armchairs—check. Centuries-old coffered ceiling and dark paneled walls—double check. A fireplace surrounded by a plain stone mantel so tall he could stand upright inside it—triple check. The white marble floors with thick black veining covered by a muted area rug in cool tones rounded out the picture, softening the hard edges, making him feel at home.

He murmured. Fire leapt from his skin, streaming across the space to land inside the grate. The smell of scorched sap and evergreen rose as the seven-foot-long log started to burn.

Ignoring the snap, crackle, and pop, he rounded the end of his desk. The Bloomberg terminal woke. Stock prices and the commodity index rolled across the double screens. Blue light poured over his keyboard, reaching out to touch the photo album sitting in front of it. An old school way to store photographs

—thick, bound by dark green leather, full of information he wanted to know and should never have read.

"Fuck," he growled, scowling at the stupid thing.

He never should've taken the album from The White Hare. Sometimes curiosity equaled disaster.

Goddamn her.

He wasn't going to make it another forty-eight hours.

Kruger knew it, had been fighting errant urges since the moment she walked into his sphere. Admitting the weakness sucked, but denying his interest never got a male anywhere. The last few hours had been torture. The need to know more about her made him itch, stoking his imagination, making him want to go back and see her again. To dissect the struggle and figure out what drew him to her.

His reaction to the she-devil defied all experience.

His eyes narrowed on the album. Fucking innkeeper. Annoying wee firebrand.

Ferguson McGilvery had accomplished what no one else ever had—wormed her way under his skin with her bad attitude, stubborn spirit, and pretty green eyes. She'd turned him inside out in less than five minutes, shaking his foundation while filling him with doubt. He'd shouted at her, for fuck's sake. Slammed his fist against her goddamned desk. Lost his cool completely, his ethics forgive him.

He didn't hurt females. He preferred charming a lass, not yelling at her...or threatening to kill her.

Kruger yanked the chair away from his desk. Fire burned holes in the leather. His magic repaired it a second before he sat down. Heavy springs whined as he leaned back, inflicting his six-foot-seven, two-hundred-and-seventy-pound frame on the innocent piece of furniture.

He frowned at the album again. The entire mess was Mavis's fault. Ferguson's godmother had screwed him over by muddying the waters. Now, the way forward lay in shambles. There was no clear path for him to follow, which made him question everything—his mission, the drive behind it, and the secret he clung to like a raft of rats fighting to stay afloat as floodwaters rolled in.

Dread settled like a stone in the pit of his stomach.

With Ferguson in the mix, he couldn't think straight. Bad news, given how high the stakes had become, and what her arrival meant in the long term.

The White Hare constituted a clear and present danger.

He'd believed Mavis to be a real innkeeper. After meeting Ferguson, he now knew the truth. Her godmother had been little more than a placeholder—a weak substitute when compared to Ferguson's magical bloodline. She was a powerhouse, a high-energy female who possessed the kind of magic that would not only connect to the life essence of the inn, but feed it.

With a full-blooded innkeeper in residence, The White Hare would grow more powerful by the day. More Magickind would be drawn to the Parkland, seeking safe space and sanctuary. The cosmic crossroads would become crowded. Aberdeen would be transformed into a hub, upping the chances he'd be discovered. Which meant, no matter how much Ferguson intrigued him, he couldn't give in...or leave her to her own devices.

His brothers-in-arms could never know. The second his pack learned the truth about him, he'd lose everything. His home. His family. His future inside the Scottish pack.

All of it hung in the balance. Every day The White Hare remained open, the risk of exposure grew. Sooner or later, one of the supernatural guests who frequented the inn would wander into town—or cross his flight path—and recognize him. Show him the wrong kind of respect. Give him the kind of due he didn't want. Make his brothers dig deeper into his past and figure out his origin.

Silfer's son, in their midst. The offspring of the arsehole responsible for Dragonkind's fall from grace and the centuries of hardship that followed.

Rolling his shoulders to break the tension, Kruger learned forward and flipped the photo album open. A mistake—he should stuff the thing back inside his mental vault and forget about it. Or better yet, return it to the bookshelf he'd taken it from inside her study.

Stealing a piece of Ferguson's history was stupid. Knowing more about her—seeing her baby pictures—only made things worse. But he'd needed to understand her background, her parental line, along with where she'd been for the better part of thirty years.

His best guess? Somewhere in America. The Midwest, probably. Her accent gave her away. Her baby book did the rest.

Her sire's name was right there, in the middle of the album, written in bold scrawl on a branch stretching out from her family tree—Icabod McCrae, eleventh innkeeper descended from the House of Antegaul.

Following the outstretched limbs, Kruger ran his fingertip over the tree, zigzagging over the collection of her ancestors. So many names, though Ferguson's wasn't there. Neither was her mother's. His eyes narrowed on the blank spaces above twisted branches. An oversight? Or had she been left unnamed for a reason?

Excellent questions. A mystery he itched to solve.

Could be her mother and sire had had a falling-out. Divorce happened all the time—even among Magickind. Could be something else, though.

Icabod McCrae hadn't let his family go by choice. The former innkeeper had shielded Ferguson by sending her away.

The last name told him a lot. Ferguson didn't share one with her sire—a point of pride for most Magickind. Bloodlines, and the traditions that accompanied them, were all-important. A male as powerful as Icabod would never have given Ferguson a different name unless absolutely necessary.

Something stunk in the Parkland. Something dangerous. Maybe even deadly, considering Ferguson's sire was no longer running The White Hare, and hadn't for thirty years. Nothing in the album explained why, and Kruger wanted to know the reason. He needed to understand—

"Shite," he said, interrupting the thought midstream.

He'd gone around the bend. Getting involved, being sucked into the mystery, was a bad idea. He wanted The White Hare shut down...period. He didn't need to unearth its history—or understand how the past affected the female driving him insane. Jumping inside that wormhole, knowing about Ferguson, would only lead to him wanting to know more...and then more after that.

With a curse, he slammed the album closed. His dragon shifted deep inside him, then balked, waking up to express his opinion.

"Bugger off," he muttered, trying to ignore the insistent nudge. "We cannae allow her tae stay. She isnae ours."

His beast bared his fangs.

"Move off it."

An acrid ripple curled through him. The rustle of scales clattered through his head. Heat prickled over his nape, then down his spine. All the reasons he must investigate further streamed through into his head. His dragon wasn't messing around, asking questions Kruger kept trying to pretend didn't exist. Things like: was Ferguson safe inside the inn? Would the forces that had eliminated her sire return now that his daughter stood in his stead? Would they try to kill her too?

"Double shite," he growled, staring at the olive branches crossed like swords stamped in green leather. "You're not going tae let it go, are you?"

His dragon snorted, forcing smoke up his throat.

Kruger blew out the toxic plume. Tasting fire and brimstone on his tongue, he sighed in resignation. Looked like he'd be breaking the agreement he made with Ferguson, upping the timeline and—

"Do you make a habit out of talking tae yerself in here?"

His attention snapped toward the open door.

Wearing a pair of black wraparounds, one shoulder braced against the jamb, Wallaig stood watching him. A sneak attack. His XO knew how to maneuver and, when he sensed something about to go awry, seldom let things lie. It didn't matter that Wallaig had lost his sight fifty years ago and couldn't see (at least, not in conventional ways). The lethal male never allowed his blindness to slow him down, turning a shortcoming that would kill most Dragonkind warriors into a strength, refusing to accept it as a weakness.

Seeing without *seeing*, his XO leveled him with a look.

Kruger tensed. Flames danced across his shoulders as his dragon reacted to the perceived threat. He doused the blaze, pretending the male's unexpected visit hadn't startled him.

Dark red hair glinting in the low light, Wallaig raised a brow. "A wee bit jumpy, arenae you?"

"Why're you up so early?" Kruger asked, deflecting.

"Felt you prowling around. Smelled the smoke and venom. Amantha's still asleep, so I came tae see what's got you in a bind."

"I'm—"

"Donnae do it."

"What?"

"Lie tae me."

"Fuck."

"Something's crawled up yer arse. Spill, laddie."

Pushing away from his desk, Kruger leaned back in his chair and looked up at the ceiling. So many straight lines. Lots of perfect angles. No scorch marks on the oak planks. A symphony of symmetry, unlike the jagged, lopsided mess inside his head. He should take Wallaig up on his invitation to talk. A smart male would accept a hand up and out of the turmoil. Holding the uncertainty in wasn't working. He couldn't wipe the slate clean and un-meet her.

Every time he told himself he could move forward without taking Ferguson's wellbeing into account, he ended up right back where he started: fucked up, confused, without the tools necessary to snip the thread, tie off the situation, and—

"It's the lass, isnae it? The innkeeper." Wallaig frowned. "What's her name?"

"Ferguson."

"Rannock says she's spectacular."

Kruger's nostrils flared. He bared his teeth, disliking the idea Rannock had been talking about her.

Wallaig huffed. "Down, boy."

"Fuck off."

"You got it bad."

"Not kidding, mon. *Fuck. Off.*"

"Rookie mistake," Wallaig murmured, the corners of his mouth twitching. "Fight it all you like, laddie—gonna be fun for the rest of us tae watch—but word tae the wise, you'll lose in the end. Once yer dragon's locked on, you're cooked. Done. No turning back or negotiating with it. Best tae accept what you cannae change, Ruger. Work it out with yer brothers, then do what needs tae be done and—"

"What? Claim her?"

"Now you're getting it."

Kruger clenched his teeth. "It isnae like that."

"You sure?"

"Aye."

"Cuz you donnae sound sure tae me."

Of course he didn't. Since the moment he left Ferguson, all he'd wanted to do was go back. Draw on her scent. Taste her. Touch her. Give her and her smart mouth something better to do than argue with him.

No way in hell he would admit it, though—or cry defeat so early in the game. He could still win. All he needed to do was figure out another plan of attack.

"I want The White Hare, not her."

Wallaig snorted.

"Unlike you, I donnae enjoy drama queens."

"My mate isnae a drama queen. She's spirited. Opinionated. Smart as hell, too. Fuck, Ruger. 'Tis shocking how bloody smart she is. Keeps me on my toes without even trying. *Me,* mon. Can you imagine?"

Not really. Well over three hundred years old, the male had seen a lot and done more. Feed his IQ into the equation, and no one ever outwitted or outmaneuvered him. The fact Amantha challenged Wallaig in ways the male found difficult to follow made their relationship all the more dynamic, all the more precious. And honestly, Kruger was happy for his friend. The male deserved the best, every ounce of contentment life offered after the loss he'd suffered fifty years ago.

"You like it," he said, studying his friend. "When she butts up against you, disagrees with you, challenges you—you like it."

"You bet yer arse I do. Hell, I tweak her tail just tae taste her fire." Pushing away from the door, Wallaig moved farther into the room. Powered by the essence of fire dragon, magic swirled into Kruger's airspace as the big male unloaded his bulk in the armchair opposite him, lifted his legs, and planted his size sixteens on the desktop. "Smart females are the most fun. The feistiest, too. Wicked hot in bed. Compelling out of it. A win-win all the way around."

A win-win. An interesting concept, one Kruger never entertained while closing business deals. His instincts ran much more lethal than that. He wanted to dominate, not compromise. He wasn't above dismantling a company to get what he wanted, the way he wanted it. Some might label that cruel. Kruger called it the way of the world: eat or be eaten. The weak or insecure didn't belong in the arena he played in every day.

Popping the sunglasses onto the top of his head, Wallaig rubbed the inside corners of his eyes, then raised his head. Damaged, stripped of color by deadly UV rays, white irises met his, except...

Kruger frowned.

Wallaig's eyes were no longer white. Not completely. His pupils looked normal now. Black. Round. No longer covered by thick film. Stranger still, patches of dark green broke through the milky layer, making his irises look like a warped checkerboard.

"Listen tae me, Ruger. It'll save you time and—"

"What the fuck?"

Wallaig's brows snapped together. "What the fuck what?"

"Yer eyes, brother."

"Yer changing the subject."

Planting his forearms on the desk, Kruger leaned forward to get a better look. Aye, no question—something had changed in the last month. Something big. Something monumental, if the return of color meant what he believed it might.

"Wallaig," he murmured. "Can you see?"

His XO's mouth curved. "It's coming back."

"Yer sight?"

"I already knew Amantha was a miracle worker. Haven't had her in my bed long, but my mate, her energy and the nourishment she feeds me... Christ, mon —extraordinary. Every time I connect with her, the pain clears and the damage lessens. Might take six months, might take a year, but little by little I'm regaining my ability tae see. My peripheral vision is almost perfect now."

Throat so tight he struggled to speak, Kruger rasped, "Bloody hell."

"I know," Wallaig said, sounding equally hoarse.

He stared at his XO, not knowing what to say. His friend stared back, suffering from the same disease—

speechlessness brought on by a gratitude so profound it burrowed into marrow and bone, rocking him soul deep.

One minute stretched into more.

Kruger cleared his throat. "Happy for you, brother. Happy you found her."

"Amantha's everything, Ruger. *Everything.*" Trying but failing to contain his emotion, Wallaig shifted in the armchair. "So listen tae me, lad. Listen carefully. I donnae know why you have such a hard-on for The White Hare, but whatever the reason—change the plan. Adjust yer goals. Come up with new ones, I donnae give a fuck. We all know you're ruthless. Everyone respects you for it, but if Ferguson is tae you what Amantha is tae me, you'll need her more than yer drive tae conqueror needs another deal."

"She may not be that tae me, Wallaig."

"You cannae sleep. You're restless, banging around the lair with yer flame burning bright. My guess? You cannae stop thinking about her. All you want tae do is return tae her," Wallaig said, nailing him with his patchwork eyes. "Time tae answer the question and find out what she means tae you."

"By what—touching her?"

"Do you want tae?"

He glared at his friend.

Wallaig's lips twitched. "Well, that answers that. So aye, lad, touch her and see what happens."

See what happens.

Fuck him, but...

Was it really that simple?

The question sparked interest so intense Kruger's fingertips started to tingle. Touching Ferguson would be a phenomenal experience. He already knew it, sensed it, craved it in ways that scared him a little. But

Wallaig was right. Avoiding the truth would not only prolong his pain, but prevent him from pivoting— from protecting Ferguson when she needed him to, so...fuck it. Decision made. He was going all in, banking on the idea he could keep his secret by winning in other ways.

Now all he needed to do was storm The White Hare, brave the wee firebrand's wrath, and test Wallaig's theory by finding out for himself.

8

J etlag gnawing on her, Ferguson sat cross-legged in the middle of the bed. New country. New time zone. New room with a fresh coat of teal-blue paint and an antique sled bed covered in a downy comforter. Tons of matching throw pillows, some with tassels and fringe, others with ruffles and frills stuffed behind her back, propping her up when all she wanted to do was fall down.

She needed sleep. Eight hours would be good, but she'd settle for one. A little respite from the relentless pace—and information overload. An understanding, if somewhat crippling, reaction. After hours spent following Hendrix around, she was tapped out, her mind crammed full, on the verge of being overwhelmed and letting the tears clogging her throat loose.

Goddamn her godmother. Along with the cryptic, crazy-ass letters.

Closing her eyes, she swayed as fatigue pressed in. Pressure built behind her eyes. Pain bloomed, buzz-sawing into a full-blown headache. She pressed the heels of her palms into her eye sockets. The letter she held rustled, the paper edge rasping against her hair, making the messy bun on top of her head wobble.

"Effing eff, eff," she muttered, doing what she always did, pivoting away from the F-word, even though the situation called for the real thing. A few of them, actually. A whole string of expletives. Maybe while she stomped around and threw things.

Winding up and letting fly would help work out her frustration. Might get rid of the anxiety clawing the inside her chest, too. She rubbed the grit from her eyes, then dropped her hands into her lap. The corners of the letter flapped. Her gaze tracked to the silver candleholders on the stone mantel.

She imagined grabbing the pair. She envisioned hurling both into the empty fireplace. She heard the crash-bang, the dent and clang. The loud sounds echoed inside her head as she turned her attention to the vase full of flowers sitting on the table next to the chaise longue.

A better solution. She could explain shattered porcelain. Easy for her to blame it on clumsiness. A broom and dustpan, a few swipes and...*voila*! Carnage erased, anxiety unleashed, no need for her to tell Hendrix and for gossip to run rampant through The White Hare.

Blinking to clear a bad case of blurry vision, Ferguson glanced at the alarm clock on the bedside table. Ten forty-seven p.m. Nearly twenty-four hours since her arrival at The White Hare, and not a wink of sleep. Or rest, never mind a moment to herself.

After Kruger's oh-so-unpleasant visit, Hendrix had ushered her into the fray, with zero regard for her newbie status. He gave her a tour of the hotel, introducing her to the staff, encouraging her to stop and chat with guests—the pride of werelions enjoying a late lunch in the dining room, the vampire lounging at the bar inside the nightclub on the basement level, the

minotaur at the front desk waiting to check in, the cy-
clops wandering down one of the many corridors.

The urge to stop and stare almost got the better of
her. Not wanting to be eaten (or maimed), she hadn't
dared, holding it together with each introduction, allowing Hendrix to show her off, battling shock as he
explained the inner workings of the inn...along with
its bizarre rules.

Without prompting, the cast-iron plaque mounted
on the wall in the main lobby surfaced in her mind's
eye.

RULES GOVERNING THE WHITE HARE & PARKLAND:

1. **No Killing Permitted** — offenders will be exe-
cuted. No exceptions.

2. **Physical Combat to Resolve Grievances is En-
couraged** — consultation with the battle guide recommended.

3. **Injury to Staff Members will Result in Immediate Expulsion**

4. **Nudity Permitted in Designated Areas Only** —
maps available upon request.

5. **The Innkeeper's Word is LAW** — disputes will
be presided over by her. All rulings are final.

FERGUSON FROWNED. Five rules. A few lines stamped
on steel. Didn't seem like nearly enough, given the violent nature of the guests who stayed at The White
Hare on a regular basis.

Case in point? The three-headed wolfhound she'd

seen prowling around the first-floor landing. Or the knot of winged snakes wrapped around the outdoor heater in a corner of the back patio. All weird, though also wonderful in a mixed-up, otherworldly kind of way.

Five rules. Just *five*. To be enforced by her. The new innkeeper who didn't have a clue what the hell she was doing. Though remembering the rules no doubt counted as a good start.

A miracle, given her current state of mind. And yet the do-not-do list—along with the other information Hendrix had imparted—stuck to her frontal lobe like plaque, prompting her to keep a running tally of the things she needed to do in the coming days, weeks, and months. Along with all the current goings-on inside the hotel.

Something she was doing...right now. Without effort. Monitoring the situation in each suite and common area. Absorbing every bit of information The White Hare fed her through magical ties. Determining what, if anything, needed to be done to keep a guest in line, or on the flip side, ensure their comfort. All while exhausted and sitting (or hiding) inside her bedroom.

Her gaze strayed back to the vase. An outlet for her exhaustion...and the freakout she sensed on her horizon. She needed some sound and fury. Mess instead of emotional meltdown.

She leaned sideways. Feather down sighed as she grabbed the alarm clock. She yanked. The plug let go of the outlet. The gentle glow of digital numbers disappeared as the cord whipped over the edge of the bedstand. With a low snarl, she hurled the innocent item across the room. Black plastic bounced on the oriental rug, then tumbled, coming to rest between the open French doors.

Resisting the urge to roll out of bed and kick it down the hall, she glared at the unharmed clock, then returned her attention to the letter in her hand. Her stomach clenched. Unease climbed behind her breastbone, making her chest feel tight. The deep ache was more than just a sore spot. It heralded an epiphany, one she wanted to ignore, but was being forced to acknowledge.

Her gaze tracked to the seal. Cream-colored paper between her index and middle fingers, she folded the top of the letter forward. Green wax pressed flat and stuck to the top of the page. Two olive branches crossed like swords stamped into its center. Her name was scrawled on the back of the sheet below the crest.

Proper. Precise. Perfectly formed loops.

Mavis's handwriting.

A carbon copy of the other letters sitting in a sloppy pile on the coverlet in front of her. Letters she'd already cracked open and read. Thirteen in all, written in the last month, the date in the top righthand corner of each one.

She'd found the bundle of correspondence after Hendrix released her from innkeeper duty, snooping through the built-in hutch in the kitchen. Why she'd looked there first, she didn't know. But the second the door to her apartment closed behind the gorgon, she'd felt the pull and gone straight to the hutch.

Bottom drawer, buried beneath tablecloths and napkins. Right where she knew Mavis's messages would be, precisely how her godmother left them.

The White Hare was to blame. At least, she thought it was the inn. Like someone whispering in her ear, the spirit who called the Parkland home told her where to go to get what she needed—a fuller scope and the bigger picture. Information Hendrix had left out.

Omissions by design? Or the inadvertent glossing over of facts?

Both good questions.

She didn't know Hendrix well yet. Maybe excitement had gotten the better of him. Maybe he'd become so caught up having a new innkeeper to impress, he skipped over important details without realizing it. Maybe he'd simply run out of time before she called it a night.

She should probably give him the benefit of the doubt. With Kruger's unexpected visit—and annoying demands—and so many other things going on, she understood her major-domo's hesitation. Hendrix no doubt planned to dole out the bad news in increments. A little here. A dollop there. Tomorrow would be soon enough for the next round...after she'd gotten a good night's sleep.

Ferguson released a pent-up breath.

Right. Sleep. Was she really back to chewing on that?

No matter how exhausted, she knew getting the recommended amount of Zs was not going to happen tonight. Closing her eyes while listening to soothing music hadn't worked. Counting sheep was a bust. The glass of warm milk hadn't helped. And forget about meditation. Her brain was buzzing, far too full to quiet any corner of it. Which left her mind free to wander in dangerous directions. Ones that took her toward the contract and the dragon warrior who'd slammed the idiotic thing down on her desk.

She sighed.

What a shame.

Kruger might be annoying, but that didn't stop her

from noticing he was beautiful. Any woman with a working libido would think so. He was the kind of man who turned heads. Tall. Broad. Intense vibe. Sharp intellect behind angled cheekbones in an arresting face. Some would be fooled by his charm. Ferguson didn't suffer any delusions. She knew who he was—a predator wrapped in a pretty package.

And yet...

He intrigued her.

Something about him urged her to take a closer look. She sensed the vulnerability behind the façade, read the hesitation in his dark eyes, saw the discomfort in the lines of his body. She pursed her lips. *Discomfort* wasn't the right word. *Desperation* fit better.

Instinct rose on cue, seconding her assessment. Yes. *Desperate.*

Desperate to win. Desperate to keep his truth hidden. Desperate for a reason, maybe even a life-threatening one. Which meant she'd read him right. Kruger had a secret—a scary one he refused to let loose—and needed The White Hare to keep it under wraps.

Her eyes narrowed as questions circled. The what, the why, and the how. What had him tied in knots? Why couldn't he come clean? How could she help? Burying problems never worked. She should know: having spent years ignoring the truth about her ex-husband and her own mistreatment, she qualified as an expert. Secrets always killed the keeper, and denial was a tricky beast. She understood the monster, knew its vicious cycle inside and out.

Until now, she'd never truly embraced her power. She'd existed, hiding in plain sight, a stranger in her own home, too afraid to let go and lean into the person she'd been born to become.

"Crap." Rubbing the sore spot between her eyebrows, Ferguson shook her head. "Crappity-crap-crap-crap."

She shouldn't want to help Kruger. His problems were his own. It wasn't any of her business, except...

That wasn't quite true.

Solving his problem meant the dissolution of hers. Once he decided owning The White Hare served no purpose, he'd move on, and she'd be free to concentrate on the inn, instead of fighting to keep from losing it.

With her in residence, the inn was no longer dormant. Alive with magic, rooted deep in the earth, the spirit of the Parkland reached out to her. She understood its language and spoke back without words. The relationship seemed to be symbiotic, a gentle give and take. Not painful, just... present, at the ready, cluing her into the shared awakening.

The inn had been in a cold, dark place for a long, long time. But after winter came the spring. New growth. Brilliant colors. Vibrant skies and cleansing rains.

Her abilities sparked inside The White Hare, sending tremors through the Parkland, allowing her to tap into something raw and elemental. Breathing deep, Ferguson opened her senses. Warmth bubbled up, heating her palms, rushing through her veins as ties that bound strengthened and the spirit she couldn't see but felt all around her hummed, welcoming her home.

Her lips curved.

The inn whispered in her ear, *"Help him."*

She frowned. "He's a dick."

"He's yours."

Figured. She'd always been a dick magnet. Exhibit

A: her ex-husband, stepfather, and malignant step-brothers.

"Help him. Help yourself," the inn said, throwing down the suggestion like a dare.

"Huh." Glancing toward the ceiling, Ferguson turned the idea over like topsoil, looking for rot underneath. "It's not a bad plan, you know."

The inn said nothing.

Setting her elbow on her bent knee, she propped her chin on her fist and stared unseeing at the empty fire grate. "I help him. He leaves me alone. At least long enough for me to figure out how to get rid of him for good."

Walls creaked as the inn groaned around her.

Busy plotting Kruger's demise, she ignored the advice. He was trouble, absolute destruction (and hotter than effing hell), but still...

An alliance with him might work.

Two birds, one stone. Hook him, keep him on the line, but at arm's length while she settled in and learned how to control her new abilities. The White Hare was right: having Kruger, and his dragon pack, at her back while she acclimated to her surroundings wasn't the worst idea.

Chewing on her fingernail, Ferguson shook her head, hating what the strategy said about her. The entire scheme smacked of deceit, but if her deception saved the inn, well then...

The ends would justify the means.

Kruger was a big boy with a nefarious purpose. He wanted to kill The White Hare. He hadn't said so, would never admit it to her, but the second he bought the property, the Parkland would die. And so would she, in one way or another. Ferguson wasn't above playing dirty. She would cheat, beg, borrow, steal, and lie to ensure Kruger never got his hands on her birthright.

She was the innkeeper, and the responsibility to protect the Parkland fell to her, so she'd play his game. Maybe even strike a deal. If her plan worked, she'd do more than just slow him down. She'd uncover the what and the why—uproot his secret, shine a light on the reason he wanted The White Hare, disarm him before he attacked her.

Underhanded in every way, but so was Kruger. He'd live. She'd get what she wanted. A win-win, no matter how you sliced it.

Sensing the inn's disapproval, Ferguson ignored the silent censure and straightened from her slouch. She rolled her shoulders. Pain prickled through her as she put the problem of Kruger aside. She had a couple of days before he darkened her door again—plenty of time to figure out how best to deal with him. In the meantime...

She refocused on the letter in her hand. Sliding her thumb over the paper, she flicked one of the corners with her nail. The creased sheet flapped in the quiet before she smoothed it all the way open. She frowned at the flawless penmanship.

Beware the Druids.

A warning, succinct and to the point. Just like Mavis.

With all her eccentricities, Ferguson's godmother had never excelled at subtlety, or did anything in half measures. Mavis had left Ferguson to fend for herself. No training. No transition period. Nary a word of advice about her duties as the new innkeeper. Just a few vague instructions written on thick stationery with a fancy crest of two olive branches that most would say symbolized harmony.

All Ferguson saw was chaos.

Proof positive lay in the other letters. One said: *Bathe naked in the Darkwood.* Another instructed: *Welcome the Haetae.* Yet another implored her to: *Dip into the midnight cauldron and embrace the moon.*

Thirteen letters. A single phrase written on each one. Nothing but nonsense that seemed to signal her godmother's recent descent into insanity. An upsetting thought, given what Mavis meant to her, and—

The soft snick sounded.

A quiet hiss of a door opening and closing.

The sound of near-silent footsteps tapping across tile.

Her attention snapped toward her bedroom door. Wide open. No protection from the intruder she sensed sneaking in through the back door.

Head tilted, Ferguson stayed still and listened. The quiet creak of floorboards came next. Moving slow and steady, she set the letter on top of the pile and, without making a sound, drew the afghan covering her legs aside. Cool air prickled over skin left bare by her pajama shorts as she shifted toward the edge of the bed.

Gaze riveted to the entrance, she reached for the cricket bat leaning against the bedside table and murmured, "Lights out."

The White Hare listened and obeyed.

The lone lamp on the nightstand winked out, plunging her room into darkness. Her hand curled around the handle of the heavy bat. Her feet touched down on the soft rug covering the wide-planked floor. Her vision flickered. Infrared blinked on. Night turned to day as abilities she didn't know she possessed flared, allowing her to see in the dark.

Perception expanded another notch. Echolocation

came online. She sent a gentle pulse out, using vibration to locate the intruder.

There. Crossing the living room. Now rounding the end of her couch.

She clenched her teeth. He was good at creeping, intent and stealth on display as he crept under an archway into a hall lined with bookcases.

Cranking an internal dial, she sharpened her focus. Big guy. Solid presence. Intense magical vibe wrapped in power so profound it preceded him out of the center vestibule, slithering into the corridor that led to her room.

Beware the Druids.

Like a well-timed antidote, Mavis's message invaded her veins.

Her heart picked up a beat. Blood throbbed in her ears. *Enemies.* She had *enemies.* Not just Kruger and the dragon pack backing him—others she didn't yet know about, but perceived in ways that stretched her abilities and weren't yet part of her repertoire.

Normal girls had normal problems. Abnormal girls ended up with crazy problems. Jethro, Cuthbert, and Luther—along with the host of other ghosts who'd visited over the years—set her firmly in the second category. Ordinary wasn't part of her make-up, so instead of fighting the flux, she bent the curve, embraced strange and, absorbing the inn's magic, made it her own.

Calm curled through her. Prickles exploded down her spine.

She heaved the cricket bat. The square tip swung up, preceding her around the end of her bed. Attention aimed at the door, she murmured her wishes. The air stilled. Quiet descended as the inn muffled her movements. Flexing her hands around the taped handle, she tiptoed toward the door.

The floorboards outside creaked.

Shifting right, she pivoted, then drifted backward. Her shoulder blades met the wall. Hidden from view, she listened as her would-be assailant paused in the corridor. Nothing but a whisper of sound and the slight stirring of air. Locked on to the guy, she closed her eyes, counting off the seconds, sensing every movement he made. Whoever he was, he was in for a rude awakening...and crushing defeat.

She might not know who he was, but she knew precisely how to deal with him. No hesitation. No holds barred. No need to consult The White Hare's battle guidelines or call in Hendrix.

The inn showed her the way as a shadowy figure moved between the jambs. Fury and adrenaline collided. Heat burned through her veins. Magic infused her muscles, lending her strength. With a snarl, she swung the cricket bat. The guy invading her room sucked in a quick breath.

Too little, too late.

She hit him with the broadside of the bat. Wood cracked against bone. A grunt exploded from his lungs, half agony, half curse.

She wound up again.

"Fuck. Wait—"

"Eff you, asshole!"

"Fer—"

Baring her teeth, Ferguson didn't listen. She heaved her weapon and, without mercy, hammered him again.

9

The first strike hammered him in the middle of his chest. The second slammed into the side of his head.

Hardwood cracked against his cheek. His chin snapped sideways. Mind-shredding sound detonated between his temples. Vision sheeting white, he felt the tear as his skin split open. A metallic scent splashed into the air. Kruger cursed and, reeling from the attack, stumbled back into the corridor.

His shoulder blades collided with a row of bookcases. One of the solid wooden shelves splintered. Pain ricocheted like automatic gunfire as books jumped over the edge, taking a nosedive toward the rug underfoot. Leather-bound volumes thumped against the floor. Pivoting to his right, he avoided another strike. Something wet dripped into his eye as his mind came back online and realization struck.

Fucking hell.

Blood. *His* blood.

He tasted it, smelled it, felt it racing through his veins, rolling hot and thick down the side of his face, dripping from the edge of his jaw.

A droplet splattered on the floor.

The fire-venom in his plasma sparked. Woolen threads burned as tendrils of flame flared in the dark, eating through the area rug to scorch the oak planks underneath.

The flash fire died out. Disbelief rolled through him.

He blinked to clear his head, then growled at the cause of his pain. The wee she-devil. She'd hit him. Nailed him hard—*twice*. With unerring accuracy, when that shite was impossible.

He was cloaked, hidden deep inside an invisibility spell. No way in hell she should've been able to hear his approach, never mind see him coming. Certainly not well enough to crack him upside the head with a cricket bat.

A cricket bat.

Off all fucking things.

His night vision sparked, giving him a clearer view of her. Look at her, the wee witch, wielding the weapon like she'd been born with one in her hand.

He bared the sharp points of his canines. Beyond ridiculous. He'd lost his edge—or his mind. Kruger didn't know which. He didn't have time to figure it out either, as Ferguson spun out of the doorway. Her outfit distracted him for a second. Dressed in nothing but skimpy short-shorts and a tight tank top, she pivoted on the balls of her bare feet. Muscles flexed under her smooth skin. Energy burned through her aura, lighting up his visual field.

Green, red, touched by a hint of gold. Incredible in its intensity. Devastating. Awe-inspiring. Beauty in motion as she dipped low then came back up, poised to strike again.

Caught in her web, he didn't react at first. He wanted to watch instead of intervene, catalog every detail. Tuck it away inside his memory to draw from another time, while he lay alone in his bed, mind churning, unable to sleep, locked in the cold, dark place he often went when silence ruled and the lair grew still. Thinking of Ferguson facing him head-on— bold and fierce, protecting her turf—would fuel his imagination and keep him warm during long nights and what seemed like endless days.

Warmth.

Goddess, he longed for it. For the ease and heat, along with the relief both would bring.

Self-preservation refused to allow the indulgence. A practiced hand, instinct came to his rescue, righting his balance, ignoring her allure, forcing him to deal with the problem at hand.

Ferguson unleashed her swing.

Kicking books out of his way, Kruger ducked.

The bat whiffed over his head.

Undeterred by the miss, she brought the weapon back around. Fast. So fucking fast. Untrained, sure, but her lack of fighting skills didn't change what he faced.

A female on the war path, she'd skipped reasonable, flown past pissed off, and sailed straight into fury. He dodged another strike. She jabbed at him, swinging the bat like a sword. The square end glanced off the top of his thigh. He grunted. She lashed out with a backhand, driving him back toward the end of the hall.

"Lass—"

"Eff you! Eff you, eff you, *eff you,* you effing jerk!"

Despite the seriousness of her reaction, Kruger's mouth curved. He shouldn't find anything funny. Nothing about the situation warranted laughter, but... bloody hell. She was magnificent. Glorious in her fierceness. Expression set, eyes flashing, bioenergy sparking, the gold in her aura flaring so bright she nearly blinded him with her brilliance.

Respect for her shot through him.

Movements smooth and quick, she came after him again.

"*Fazleima*, stop," he murmured, hands up, retreating as she advanced.

Deep in her rage, unable to see reason, she took another swipe at him. The thin edge of the square bat whistled through the air. Kruger jumped back. A swing and another miss.

Gaze riveted to her, he shifted sideways, then reversed course and pivoted the other way. A tactic designed for one purpose—to force her to move in the direction he dictated instead of the one she wanted. In full retreat, he watched her take the bait and begin mirroring his movements, knowing she was giving him the upper hand.

He clenched his teeth, not liking what he'd done... or was about to do. "Fergie—"

"Don't call me that!"

"Sweetheart—"

"Go to hell!"

His fault. Her reaction, the fallout, was *his fault*.

He'd invaded her space without giving her a heads-up. For the second time in twenty-four hours.

The first time he'd wanted to unsettle her, to drive home a point—he wouldn't allow her to stand in his way. This visit, however, something far more dangerous drove him. Compulsion, the need to know, had taken hold. So he'd done what he never had before and changed course, shoved ambition aside and made another plan. Unprecedented, given his nature, but

Wallaig wasn't wrong: Kruger needed to know why he reacted to Ferguson the way he did.

Had his reaction been amplified by the heat of the moment?

Was he imagining how he'd felt when he looked at her?

Or was his attraction driven by something else altogether?

Excellent questions that needed to be answered. Which left him with two options: respect the agreement he made with Ferguson and wait the requisite seventy-two hours before approaching her again. Or... execute a fast landing at The White Hare after sundown, infiltrate the innkeeper's apartment while she slept, take a quick peek, disprove Wallaig's theory, then rejoin his brothers-in-arms on the hunt.

Short, sweet, simple. He'd needed a couple of minutes. Five tops. Hardly any time at all to untangle the mystery she presented. Just long enough to take his own temperature, examine his response to her without anger fogging the lens to discover if what Wallaig suspected held true.

What he managed to achieve instead was unconscionable.

He'd frightened her.

Her expression conveyed the message. The tears shimmering in her eyes did the rest, prompting him to run through his options. Trying to talk her down wouldn't work. Avoiding her attempts to maim him wasn't getting him anywhere either. But he couldn't allow her to continue. He needed to shut Ferguson down before she hurt herself.

Attuned to her bioenergy, Kruger read her fatigue and saw the crash coming. Exhaustion hung like a noose around her neck, pulling tighter with every swing she took. She stood on the edge, on the verge of going over, and yet continued attacking. He kept dodging and, even knowing it wouldn't help, talked to her in soothing murmurs. He swung each like a weapon, listening to her breath hitch, watching her muscles strain, looking for an opening as he timed his intervention.

Yanking the bat away wouldn't work. Magic had fused her hands to the handle, lending her strength, making the bat an extension of her body. If he took it away without her letting go, he'd peel the flesh from her fingers.

Dancing the dance, he allowed her to back him into a rectangular vestibule with high ceiling and mosaic tile underfoot. A large skylight looked down from above. Weak light ghosted through the glass panel, playing in dark corners, casting shadows, making the coppery tendrils of Ferguson's hair glow.

He retreated another step, entering the open space completely. Fast-moving clouds above the inn parted. Moon-glow spilled through the skylight, anointing wainscoting painted bright white. His night vision shuttered, protecting his light-sensitive eyes as Ferguson raised the cricket bat again. Moving fast, she attacked quick, charging over the lip of the hall into the vestibule.

Fighting stance set, he counted off the seconds. Three, two, one...

The cricket bat sliced toward him.

He grabbed the wooden edge, arresting it mid-swing. She snarled. He murmured in response, hoping to soothe her. The tactic didn't work. Not that he'd expected it to. As she yanked, trying to loosen his grip, Kruger tugged her off balance, reached out, and shackled her other wrist. His palm met her pulse point. Her bioenergy spiked, curling up his forearm. Pleasure slammed through him. His dragon growled in approval. Biting down on a groan, he shoved aside his beast's reaction to stay on track and, with gentle twist, shoved her arm behind her back.

"Son of a bitch!"

"Calm, *fazleima*. You're all right."

"Eff you."

"Anytime you like, Fergie. I'm game."

She hissed at him.

He picked her up. As her feet left the floor, he secured his hold and yanked her toward him. Air puffed from her mouth as her breasts collided with his chest. Tendrils of powerful energy sparked. Heat licked over his skin as the Meridian surged, opening a channel deep inside him. Sucked into the sensory vortex, he shivered as energy-fuse clicked into place like a missing puzzle piece, tying him to her, and her to him.

Son of a bitch was right. Goddess. Unbelievable. She felt so good pressed against him. Without effort, she tore him open. In the same instant, she put him back together, invading his mind, settling into his blood and bones, connecting to his life force, giving him something he hadn't known he was missing— connection, peace, perfect magical pitch, the kind of resonance he hadn't known existed. Or thought possible.

Not for him. He never embraced interpersonal connections. His bloodline and violent nature ensured he stayed on the outside looking in. But Ferguson...

Bloody hell. She was perfection. Attitude tangled up with a gentleness he sensed beneath her surface but had yet to see in action. Goddess, how he wanted that. Her acceptance. Her bold, fearless spirit. All of her affection directed at him, so he could return it.

She squirmed against him. Electrostatic current licked over his skin. Heat pooled in his groin. His dragon snarled, happy to have any part of her touching him. She tried to head-butt him. Tucking his face into the side of her neck, he waylaid the attempt without bruising her, then spun around. A couple of short strides, and he brought her in for a soft landing against the wall.

"Shit." Rearing in his arms, she yanked on the cricket bat. "Let go."

"You first," he said, pressing the flat of the bat against the wood paneling.

"You—"

Kruger flexed his fingers around her wrist, reminding her he had her arm pinned to the small of her back. Her eyes widened. She stilled as the full extent of her peril registered. Nose to nose with her, he watched up close as she blinked. Thick copper-red lashes, framing eyes so green he struggled to name the color. Not evergreen. Not leaf or brilliant grass green. Not even close to moss green, though—

"Kruger..." A whispered word. A hitch in her voice. Fear in her scent, tinging her aura smoky gray as a quiver shook her frame.

Hearing her uncertainty, he locked down his reaction, but refused to back away...or let her go. Not yet. Not until the lesson he wanted her to learn sank in. He wanted to make sure she understood the message he was sending. No chance for misunderstandings. No breakdowns in communication.

His hold on her firm, but gentle, he drew away slowly. His gaze met and bored into hers. "You feel me?"

Her throat worked as she swallowed. "Yes."

"Do you understand?"

A slight shake of her head. "No."

Well, at least she was honest. Most females in her position would agree just to agree, in the hopes of placating him.

"See me, feel me, hear me, Fergie. I'm not going tae hurt you. Not now, not ever, lass."

"You've got me pinned. My feet aren't touching the floor."

"Am I hurting you?"

She took a breath, opened her mouth, and—

"Donnae lie."

Her teeth clicked together as she snapped her mouth shut. Lips pursed, she thought about it a second. Her expression turned mulish. "No."

"No what?"

"You aren't hurting me."

"I know."

"Then why ask?"

"Needed tae hear you say it. Realize it for yourself," he said, tone soft, relaying his message the only way he knew how—with actions. "Absorb the truth of that, *fazleima*. Take it in. It's important."

Wariness flared in her eyes. "I thought you didn't like me."

"I never said that."

An adorable little V formed between her brows. "You're early. You said I had three days. What's going on?"

"Let the weapon go, and I'll explain."

"Put me down first."

"Nay." Unable to deny his need, Kruger dipped his head. His cheek brushed against hers. She sucked in a quick breath. He nestled in, pressing his mouth to the hinge of her jaw. Inhaling deep, he filled his lungs with her scent. A low sound left him. Goddess, nirvana. She smelled amazing. So fucking sweet he forgot where he stood for a moment.

"What are you doing?"

"Scenting you."

"*Scenting* me?"

"You smell phenomenal."

"And you're effing crazy."

The comment forced a chuckle from his throat. His temple rubbed against hers, sending gorgeous sensation sparking down his spine. "Probably, but that doesnae change the fact you smell good."

She huffed. "Back off."

"Let go of the bat."

"I would, but..."

"But what?"

"I can't. It's... I think maybe it's stuck."

"Stuck?"

"To my hand. You're going to have to take it away from me."

"I'll injure you if I do. You need tae power down, lass."

"Power down?" she asked, sounding confused.

"Yer magic's frothing. The handle's fused tae yer palm. Take a deep breath and power down. You need tae let go of yer own accord." Keeping her pinned with her feet a foot off the floor, he slid his hand down the length of the cricket bat. Smooth wood turned to rough tape at the handle. Fitting his hand over hers, he mimicked her grip, pressing his fingers over her much smaller ones. "Power down, Ferguson."

A pause. A delicate shiver, then...

"I don't know how."

Surprised by the admission, Kruger retreated until he had her eyes, then tapped into her bioenergy. Perfect pitch. Just the right frequency. Pure power boosted by unerring amplification. No wonder he loved being inside the Parkland so much. Ferguson's bioenergy and The White Hare's magic were one and the same. Both vibrated at the same frequency. Her abilities fueled the inn, and the beauty of energy-fuse ensured his magic nourished his mate, forming a perfect bond. One he'd felt each time he visited the inn.

The spirit of the Parkland had welcomed him from the beginning, allowing him free rein inside her boundaries as a substitute for Ferguson. As a way of connecting to the right frequency of electrostatic current until Ferguson arrived and gave it what it needed to heal.

His dragon had known all along, flying him into the Parkland often, wanting to be in the place he sensed his mate belonged.

Goddess almighty, he was an idiot. He didn't know how he'd missed so much, never mind what to do with the information now. True to form, Wallaig hadn't been wrong. Ferguson met and matched Kruger in every way, signaling something he wanted to deny, but his beast refused to ignore. The new innkeeper belonged to him. He belonged to her, which left him with one hell of a mess.

His brows snapped together.

What in the fuck was he supposed to do now?

He wanted The White Hare shut down, dormant and uninhabitable, not waking up after three decades of near-slumber.

But with Ferguson in residence, the hotel would act like a beacon and draw Magickind from all over the world. A serious problem, given the secret he needed to keep. No one could know his bloodline. *No one.*

And yet he already foresaw the unraveling, could

feel the awakening and magical rift opening as the inn responded to the female in his arms. Connected to her, he felt the Parkland align with Ferguson, plug itself in and draw on her power, beginning the arduous task of repairing decades of damage in order to restore balance.

Growth and renewal precipitated by his mate. A female he was now duty-bound to protect. Which brought him to the main problem...

Destroying The White Hare would mean hurting her. If he did what he needed to ensure his own protection, the Parkland would die. If the Parkland died, his mate would suffer terrible magical withdrawal, the kind most Magickind never survived.

"Fucking hell."

"Kruger?"

"Goddamn it."

"Are you all right?"

"Nay, I'm not all right," he said between clenched teeth.

"What's wrong?"

"Beside the fact you're a pain in the arse?"

"You're not so hot yourself, you know?"

"Bullshite, *fazleima*. You think I'm hot."

She scowled at him. "Can you stop being annoying, so we can get on with it?"

"On with what?"

"Hellooo," she called, as though he stood across the apartment instead of an inch away. "Bat stuck to my hand...remember that eensy-weensy problem?"

His lips twitched. His mate was fucking hilarious. "Forgot for a second."

"What?"

"That you're a newbie. A virgin."

She jolted against him. "I'm not a virgin."

"In my world, you are. You've no idea how to use yer magic, do you? You've never had tae before."

"What are you doing here, anyway?" she asked, bristling with irritation. "How the hell did you get in?"

"The hotel let me in."

"No, it didn't."

"It absolutely did. I jogged up the steps, and the door swung right open."

"But—"

"The White Hare wants me here," he murmured, delighted when she wrinkled her nose. His mate had no clue how to hide her reactions. She broadcasted her thoughts, the nuance in her expression so honest she gave him everything without realizing he read her without difficulty. She was a contradiction, prickly on the outside, sweet on the inside. "It likes me."

Her scowl grew fiercer. "Well, I don't."

"Liar."

"Arrogant."

"Only when I'm right."

"Which you think is all the time," she snapped, watching him shrug.

"You ready?"

"To kill you?—Absolutely."

Unable to contain his amusement, he laughed again.

She stared, her lips parting as she listened to him.

"Deep breath, *fazleima*." Hilarity dying down to chuckles, he flexed his fingers, squeezing the back of her hand. She startled, then glanced sideways. He followed her lead, looking at the bat pressed to the wall. "Follow my movement. We're gonna uncurl one finger at a time. On three..."

She drew in a breath. "One."

"Two," he murmured.

"Three."

"Go."

Looking at their hands, Kruger set his forehead against hers and lifted his thumb. She made a pained sound as hers followed his, unpeeling from the handle. Some of the tape came away with it, remaining embedded in the pad of her finger, highlighting blisters that looked angry and sore.

"Fuck," he growled. "Worse than I thought."

"Next one," she said, index finger twitching beneath his.

"Rip it off. Like a plaster, aye?"

Taking another deep breath, she nodded.

Kruger opened his hand, trying to block out her pain. His strategy didn't work. He registered her sharp inhalation, felt every tremor, heard each whimper she locked between her teeth as he pulled her hand from the hilt. With a low curse, she curled into him. Wrapping her calf around the back of his knee, she turned her head into the side of his throat. A tendril of her hair stroked his jaw. Cradling her closer, he set his mouth to her crown, reveling in the softness, absorbing her pain as the cricket bat clattered to the floor.

"Ouch," she whispered.

"Give it a second, lass."

Desperate to confront her, he tucked her injured hand into his palm. He murmured, opening her clenched fist one finger at a time, then laced his through hers. Her damaged palm met the calloused surface of his. She flinched. He called on his magic, feeling the rising swell as his dragon greeted the moment, providing what his mate needed.

Heat bubbled through his veins.

The fine hairs on his nape stood on end as powerful energy swirled through him. Gentling the stream, he grabbed the current by the tail. He looped it up, around and over, then turned it toward Ferguson and let the stream loose. Heat suffused the center of his palm. Strung tight, she quivered as his magic went to work, washing away her pain, bathing her in warmth, knitting her skin back together.

Seconds ticked into more.

Ferguson released a pent-up breath.

"Better?"

"Yes."

Keeping hold of her injured hand, he fed her more healing energy as he let her wrist go. Wrapping his arm around her, he curled her closer. Her lashes fluttered, brushing his jaw as she opened her eyes. She raised her head. His gaze met hers. Caught in the moment, Kruger leaned in and kissed her. Softly. Sweetly. A barely there brush of mouths without expectation or fear of reprisal if she chose to turn away.

His teeth grazed her bottom lip.

Shock flared in her eyes.

Need for her running riot, he flicked her with the tip of his tongue. A wee taste with huge impact. His heart thumped. His focus sharpened. Watching her closely, he nipped her gently, waiting for her to react. He expected her to pull away, tell him no. Maybe even try to head-butt him again for crossing the line.

Ferguson surprised him instead, stealing his breath, giving it back, rocking him to the depths of his soul.

10

H ead warring with her heart, she breathed in as Kruger breathed out. Shared air. Shared space. Shared knowledge that something big was happening —a thing so huge Ferguson felt it overflow and tumble through her. Tendrils of heat unfurled low in her belly. A shock wave detonated inside her mind, opening channels, unlocking secret passageways, revealing hidden recesses.

Ordinary fell beneath the wave, revealing extraordinary, laying the truth bare.

She wanted him.

Really *wanted* him.

Not in a sleep-with-him-once-never-see-him again throwaway night. In a longing-to-make-him-hers-keep-him-forever kind of way. The most dangerous type. The sort that gave a girl ideas. Which always ended badly—at least for her. With heartbreak followed by five days of excessive brownie eating and the emptying of tissue boxes during a bad movie marathon.

Kruger kissed her again, softly, sweetly, inviting her in, obliterating good sense, killing her will to resist, making her tingle in interesting places.

"Kruger," she whispered, struggling to find firm footing.

"Right here, lass."

"Shouldn't we..."

"What?"

"I don't know—talk?"

His mouth brushed hers again.

A tremor shook her, clawing through her resolve. Talking first, before she went any further, was a good idea—the best, given their rough start, his plans for The White Hare, but... God. She didn't want him to put her down and back away. Didn't want to be reasonable. For once, she wanted to take instead of give. Be selfish. Be irresponsible. Be wild, live a little instead of denying what she needed.

She should pump the brakes. Stop and rethink. Change course by asking Kruger to give her some space. Ignoring the problem wouldn't make it go away. Backing off was the smart thing to do. The best way forward, given—

"*Fazleima.*"

Pitch perfect, the gorgeous undertones of his voice dove beneath her skin, making her twitch like a tuning fork. The issues on the forefront of her mind drifted into the background. The heat in Kruger's eyes did the rest, arresting her bid for self-preservation.

God help her. She couldn't do it, couldn't tell him no or deny herself the pleasure. The urge to know him was simply too strong, bubbling up, wiping her slate clean as curiosity took hold. She wanted to know everything about him: his wants and needs. His hopes and dreams. What drove him. What hurt him. What he looked like when he woke each day and went to bed each night.

Instinct urged her to lean in, so she did, leaving

safe behind as she raised her hand and cupped his jaw. Day-old stubble rasped against her skin. The full curve of his bottom lip stroked the pad of her fingertip. His breath hitched. She didn't stop, tracing his features with an attention to detail, memorizing him, feeling his intensity, loving the strength of his arms around her.

Desire fired in his dark eyes.

Caught fast, she kissed him the same way he had her, softly, answering the questions he asked without saying a word—*Do you want me, can I come closer, will you accept me...*

Am I enough for you?

That last one sealed her fate.

She knew what being unwanted felt like, understood the vulnerability and the pain. Caught in the confusion, she'd languished for years, believing the failure was her fault. Hers to own. Hers to bear. Hers to suffer through and accept. She sensed the same belief in Kruger, in his kiss and the tentative touch of his tongue. She'd asked the same questions during her marriage, doubting her own worth, wondering why other women found what she never had—a man who loved and wanted her. In bed, and out of it too.

Tracing one of his eyebrows, she held his gaze and made a decision: time to start over, to give him a shot at redemption and herself the benefit of the doubt. A scary limb to climb out on, given intuition had never been her friend. She'd made huge mistakes, taken the wrong path then stayed on it for years, allowing the people in her life to tear her down instead of tearing herself away.

Something about Kruger, though, told her she was in the right place. Finally on the right road. No longer fighting fate, but working with it.

She belonged here. Inside the inn, held secure in his arms, about to take a leap, knowing she had nothing to fear. Not from him. Not right now.

Go forward. Move back. The decision was hers.

Kruger was waiting for her.

Silence swelled, invading her bones, making her quiver as she drew in courage. Her mind reached for his. He met her halfway, pressing in, flooding her senses as she tested the connection she shared with him. It lived and breathed, winding its way, finding a path, infusing her with certainty. It was bold and brash, picking her up, carrying her away as heat sparked in her veins and the future formed in her mind's eye, showing her the way.

The second she trusted and opened up, Kruger would too.

She trailed her fingers over his cheekbone.

He murmured, half hum, part purr.

"Hi," she said, deciding starting over meant introducing herself. The right way. The way it ought to have gone the first time she met him. "I'm Ferguson. My friends call me Fergie. I'm new here. Just moved and started a new job. An important one. I'm feeling a little lost and a lot scared 'cause it's all new to me and I don't know what I'm doing yet. I like strong coffee, dark chocolate, and kissing, not necessarily in that order. Who're you?"

"Kruger," he whispered. "Venomous earth dragon. A warrior. Part of a powerful Dragonkind pack. I call the Highlands home. Have all my life, and until five minutes ago, I didnae know I'd been waiting for you tae arrive for the entirety of it."

"Yeah?"

"Aye." He kissed her again, a gentle touch before he pulled away. "I drink scotch, not coffee. Prefer the stock market tae dark chocolate. I love kissing, blow jobs, and—"

A startled laugh escaped her.

He smiled. "—lazy afternoons in bed with bonnie redheads."

"You do that a lot?"

"Never have before. Plan tae do it often with you."

His words hit her somewhere deep, plunging into places she'd never allowed anyone to touch. "I like lazy afternoons."

"Aye?"

"Absolutely, but we've still got problems."

"Not right now."

"You don't think so?"

"The morrow's soon enough tae smooth out the wrinkles, lass."

Her mouth curved.

The red rimming his outer irises sparked, making his dark eyes shimmer. "You gonna take me tae bed, Fergie?"

"I'm thinking about it."

"Think faster."

She huffed in amusement, feeling lighter than she had in ages. His desire for her pierced through, hitting her deep, somewhere profound, knitting open wounds together, filling the empty spaces inside her. Kruger was right: tomorrow would be soon enough to solve problems and bridge the distance between differences. Tonight belonged to her, to the man in her arms and exploration. For discovery and pleasure...all he could give her, every bit she could give in return.

Yes.

Absolutely.

Tomorrow was soon enough.

Shifting against him, she embraced the rise toward

anticipation, reveling in the yearning he didn't bother to hide. He put it all on the table—his desperate need for closeness, the unspoken plea for deeper connection, the patience he showed as color burnished the ridges of his cheekbones. Desire thundered through her. Kruger answered the call as blistering need threatened to pull her under.

God, he was beautiful. Strong in all the right ways...and some of the bad ones too.

Fingertips skimming, she traced his face again. His eyelashes flickered. His body tightened. Hard muscles flexed around her as he told her what he wanted. She pressed her thumb to the corner of his mouth. He opened for her. She swept in, kissing him deep, but gentle, taking her time.

A slow burn. A devastating duel. Incredible amounts of pleasure. Tongues dancing. Breath mingling. Bodies pressed close. Left hand still laced with his, she tangled the other in the dark strands of his hair. Thick. Soft. Long enough for her to grip. Beauty incarnate as he angled his head and growled down her throat, making the already fantastic absolutely phenomenal.

She took her time tasting him.

Kruger didn't rush her. Letting her explore, he pulled her away from the wall. "Wrap me up."

She hummed and did as she was told. Unlacing her fingers from his, she circled him with her arms and wrapped her legs around his hips. A pleased rumble left his throat. A hum of pleasure left hers. He turned and walked out of the vestibule into the hallway, providing friction right where she needed it. Tingles spread, shivering over her skin. Unable to hold back, she rode his edge, rolling her hips, moving with his strides, heart beating to his pulse.

"Fuck. Needy," he growled against her mouth. "How long's it been?"

"A while." *A long while, ages.* Though no way would she tell Kruger that, or admit the reason why.

"I'll make you come quick, then." His hands roamed over her back. One went high to cup her nape, dragging her tank top up with it. The other drifted low, sliding beneath the waistband of her shorts. His heated palm trailing over her skin—astounding. The snag and drift of callouses over the curve of her bare ass—fabulous.

She squirmed against him. "Hurry."

"Fingers and mouth first, *fazleima*. Get my taste. Settle you down, give you want you need, so I can fuck you slow."

"Quick first, then—"

"Nay, Fergie. I'm gonna take my time."

"I don't know if I can handle slow."

"Yer gonna have tae tonight."

"You always get your way?"

"Aye."

"We'll see," she murmured, picking up the gauntlet he'd thrown down.

He grinned against her lips. "You think you can change my mind?"

"I'm gonna try."

"Good luck with that, *fazleima*."

"Game on, cowboy."

He chuckled.

She went to work, invading his mouth, kissing him deep, determined to drive him over the edge. She wanted him fast the first time, needed to feel him all around and deep inside her. He'd get his way the second—or maybe the third—go-round...not a moment before.

A test of wills, hers against his.

A contest she planned to win as she helped him arrive at a crucial realization: give and take was better than absolute control. His dominant nature meant she had her work cut out for her, but given the prize, Ferguson was more than willing to put in the effort. Kruger needed to learn what he didn't yet know.

No matter how strong, he wouldn't always get his way. Not with her. Not tonight, or tomorrow either, during the all-important problem-solving session.

It was tricky terrain for her to navigate. Enough to break her if Kruger refused to bend and the connection growing between them cracked, shattering her heart along with it. The intensity of what she already felt for him told her it was possible. Past experience warned her it was more than probable. Sex too fast, too soon, messed with people's heads, making them do stupid things.

She knew it, believed it, but refused to stop, putting herself on the line with the understanding it could all go wrong. And in the end, she'd be forced to choose between the mesmerizing man in her arms and her duty to The White Hare.

11

Lost in carnal fog with Ferguson in his arms, Kruger kicked books out of his way. Heavy volumes tumbled across the floor. Ignoring the thuds, he turned out of the corridor and entered her bedroom. Soft lips pressed against his. Long legs wrapped around his waist. Breasts pressed to his chest. Small hands buried in his hair, fingers clenched, holding him tight as he walked and she tilted her head, taking the kiss deeper.

He groaned.

With a hum, she backed off, making him chase her mouth, driving the pace to the point of no return.

Not that he was going to stop. She was beautiful. Unabashed in her desire, uncaring she showed him her need. So fucking hot she pushed him to new heights, shredding his control, urging him to fall in with her plans and abandon his own.

He growled a warning.

She shifted against him, perfecting their fit as he tightened his grip on her. One hand cupping her arse, the other fisted in her hair, he gentled the kiss, trying to slow her down...and get his bearings.

Her bedroom was new to him. He hadn't been able

to enter during his first visit. Not that he hadn't attempted to circumvent the inn's magic. Scruples weren't his forte—principles only got a male so far, after all—but The White Hare had held the line, refusing to open the doors and allow him entry, protecting the sacred space the new innkeeper would sleep inside, pressing its point home: he wasn't welcome without an invitation.

A lot had changed in twenty-four hours.

Crossing the threshold with Ferguson in his arms, he felt the shift from nasty get-the-hell-out to warm hum. The inn liked him right where he was: inside her private sanctuary with her in his arms. Ferguson did too, encouraging his possession with soft gasps and roaming hands, caressing his shoulders, his jaw, his temples, the sensitive spots behind his ears, touching as much of him as she could reach.

Ankles locked against his lower back, she rolled her hips, riding him with firm pressure as he walked her closer to the bed. A sled-shaped frame—nothing to tie her to as he got what he needed: her naked beneath him, legs spread, busy hands unable to touch him while he shoved her agenda aside and carried on with his own. He wanted to sink into her heat, take her slow, push her hard, watched her expression when he made her come.

Normally not a problem for him.

Desperate for the pleasure he promised, the females he took to his bed always followed his lead. He'd never come up against one with a will as strong as his own. Not until now. Ferguson was threatening his control. The soft sounds she made undid him. The way she whispered his name shook him, lying waste to his convictions. Goddess, her voice. Husky with need, urgent with desire, stripped of artifice, leaving him exposed and wanting and—

Her teeth tugged at his bottom lip.

"Fergie," he said, his voice rougher than hers, but no less desperate. "Need you tae help me out here."

"No way."

"*Fazleima*—"

"Take this off." She yanked the hem of his shirt from the waistband of his jeans. "Off."

"Baby—"

"Off!"

"Hold on, lass. Let me—"

"I can't wait."

"Fergie—"

"I need your skin against mine. I *need* it, Kruger."

A tremor crept into her tone, rattling him. Unbridled urgency in her scent. Heady desperation in each word. A need so profound, he struggled against the onslaught. His dragon answered the call without his permission. Magic fizzled in his veins. His clothes disappeared into his mental vault, leaving him bare-arsed in her arms.

"God, you feel good," she whispered, hands roaming his back. Tucking her face beneath his jaw, she licked over his pulse point. He groaned in appreciation. She nipped him, keeping up the sweet torture, driving him closer to the edge of his control. "So good, handsome. Give me more."

Pleasure ignited an inferno. Heat slammed against good intentions. He locked his muscles and...bloody hell. He was doomed, so lost in her he flew past reason straight into insanity. All of a sudden, he couldn't tell her no. *No* was no longer part of his vocabulary. He could fight it. Wanted to fight it, but...

She wanted him inside her. Which meant he'd already lost the battle, bowing to her wishes as the desire to please her took him under. Ferguson needed him. He must provide what she asked—a hard, fast fucking the first time around—instead of doing what he wanted and taking his time.

"All right, gorgeous," he said, giving in, upping his pace, heading toward the bed.

His foot bashed into something. Twin points of pain slashed across his shin. An electrical cord tangled around his ankle. He stumbled sideways.

"Ignore it," Ferguson whispered.

Righting his balance, he growled, "What the fuck was it?"

"Alarm clock." The sharp edge of her teeth scraped over the sensitive spot behind his ear. A quake rumbled through him. Soft lips drifted across his skin. Her round arse filled his hands. Energy sparked everywhere she touched, making him vibrated in her arms. "Ignore it."

"I'm going tae tan yer arse."

"Before or after you fuck me?"

"Jesus, lass."

Knowing she was about to get her way, she raised her head. Green eyes full of mischief met his. He braced, preparing for more bratty behavior. She didn't disappoint: trusting him to support her weight, she leaned backward, fisted her hands in her tank top, and whipped it over her head. The messy bun atop her head let go. Her hair tumbled around her shoulders, coppery strands wanton as she flicked her hand.

Pale blue cotton landed on a standing lamp across the room, making it wobble as his gaze dipped. Air left his lungs in a rush. Fucking hell. No bra. Smooth skin and full breasts on display. His mouth watered.

"Goddess. Gorgeous, baby."

"More. I need—"

"Shh." Stroking up her spine, he fisted his hand in her hair. "Let me look at you."

Holding her firm, he took his time and looked his fill. Color spread along her cheekbones. Her eyelashes flickered. Memorizing the need in her eyes, he burned the sight of her into his brain. He tugged on the thick strands wound around his hand. Her chin came up. Her breasts rose and fell on rasping gasps. He nipped the underside of her jaw, then dipped his head.

His mouth skimmed her throat, over her collarbone and down. He curled his tongue around her nipple, swirling, teasing, making her squirm, showing no mercy. She moaned his name. Satisfaction rumbled through him. Finally. Fucking *finally*. Full curves, gorgeous female, his mate, completely in his control. Every inch of her *his*. His to fuck and please. His to claim and call his own. All of her waiting for him to give her what she needed.

With a growl, he kissed the inside curve of her breast, then turned his attention to its twin. Her nails scraped his scalp as her legs tightened around him. Shivering, on the verge of begging, she arched, pressing her heat harder against him.

His teeth grazed her.

"God."

"My name, Fergie." He nipped her. A gentle reprimand, one designed to send her higher. "You say my name while my mouth's on you."

He swirled his tongue around her nipple. Her hips bucked. Kruger sucked harder, pressing the tip against the roof of his mouth.

She moaned.

He lifted his head. "What do you call me?"

"Kruger."

"Again."

"Kruger," she gasped as he switched sides, licking her before treating her to the edge of his teeth. "*Kruger.*"

"Beautiful, *fazleima*. You're so bloody beautiful."

Her breath hitched.

"Though I'm still gonna teach you a lesson."

"For what?"

"Being bad. Playing dirty. Not listening."

"Cowboy—"

"Prepare, lass. Time for you tae beg."

She opened her mouth to object.

Giving her no time, he took her mouth and, with quick strides, moved to the bed. Instead of laying her down on the mattress, he shoved the bench at the end of the bed aside and set her arse on the footboard, the perfect height for what he planned. He had no need for softness. Not at present. His mate hadn't earned it yet.

"Brace, Fergie." Keeping her perched on the edge, he pressed in.

Off balance with her legs spread and feet dangling, she clutched at his shoulders. "What the—"

He shoved her backward. Her shoulder blades landed on the duvet cover. Her hips stayed high, putting her at a disadvantage, without leverage, as he yanked at the tie holding her pajama shorts up. A quick tug, and he stripped her bare, then stepped between the spread her knees. Her lips parted in shock. He caressed the red curls shielding her heat and, using his thumbs, opened her to his touch. Unable to wait for her to adjust, he put his mouth on her.

Ferguson arched, hips jerking in his hands.

Growling, he held her down and ate, sucking on her clit, licking into her folds, feeling her clench around his tongue. Each of her breaths came in rasping gasps. Showing no mercy, he drove her up the sharp edge of pleasure. She moaned his name. He delved deeper, giving her more, pushing her hard, already so addicted to her taste he wanted to stay right where he was...forever. *For-fucking-ever.* Until she begged him to fuck her, and he could no longer deny her.

"Kruger—"

"Ambrosia, baby. So fucking good."

"You need... I can't... Oh, *God*," she moaned.

"Slick. Jesus, so fucking slick." Needing more, he explored her with his fingers as he sucked on her clit. He lashed the tight bud with the flat of his tongue, drinking her cream, memorizing how she felt and looked and smelled. "Beauty, *fazleima*. Pure beauty."

"Shit," she rasped, planting her heels on his shoulders. She pressed up as he thrust in, using his fingers to fuck her. "Kruger, I'm gonna...I'm—"

Two fingers buried inside her, he pressed on a sensitive spot, stalling her orgasm.

"No," she moaned. "Don't."

"Not yet, *fazleima*. Not without permission."

"I... what..."

Curling his hand over the top of her thigh, he licked her again. And again. Light flicks, gentle strokes, enough to keep her on edge without sending her over.

"Oh, no."

He smiled against her folds.

"What? Oh, God..." A quiver racked her. "Wh-what?"

"Ask me, Ferguson. I want you tae ask me."

"Please," she said without a moment's hesitation.

"Please, what? Give me the words."

She clenched around his fingers, telling him she liked the way he played.

"Please, let me come."

He kissed her curls, then circled her with the tip of his tongue. "Should I give you permission?"

"I'm being good."

"Aye, you are, baby. So fucking good."

"*Please*," she begged, so tense she began to tremble.

"Such a good girl," he murmured, applying more pressure.

Her hips rolled. She keened his name.

"Come for me, Fergie."

She obeyed, exploding around him.

Sucking her clit hard, he moved his fingers. A slick retreat, and a hard thrust. He finger-fucked her over the edge, listening to her go: each hitching breath, all her hoarse whimpers as her core clenched, and he stood, lifted her off the footboard, planted her back in the bed, and followed her down. He landed on her, hips between her thighs. Still coming, she threw her head back and pressed her hips up. Mouth open, chin tipped up, she curled her legs around him and pulled him in tight, lost in the pleasure he gave her.

Wrapping his hand around her raised knee, he spread her wider. Notched tight to her entrance, he planted one forearm on the bed and growled her name. Her lashes fluttered a second before she tipped her chin down and opened her eyes.

Green eyes full of pleasure and shock. Lips parted on his name. His world settled, heart beating hard, soul sighing in bliss as he cupped her face.

"Kruger?"

"I'll give you what you need," he murmured, pressing forward. "Fuck you hard."

"Cowboy—"

He took her in a single stroke, driving so deep he touched her womb. Hot. tight. Her, him...a perfect fucking fit. What he needed, but had never known he wanted. Connection and chemistry. Primal instinct soothed by acceptance. Sex combined with fun. Someone that fit him in all ways. A female to call his own. More than a dream come true, Ferguson surpassed all expectations. She was *everything*. His end-all and be-all, every star in his stormy sky.

Gaze locked on hers, rooted deep, he circled his hips.

"Yesss, Kruger." Euphoria sharpened her features. Her limbs tightened around him. "Beautiful. You feel beautiful."

"Goddess," he groaned, surrounded by her heat, overcome by delight.

Pure bliss, every inch of her.

Another tremor knifed through her.

He kissed her, caressed her, worshiped her as he started to ride. With another whispered "yes," she raised her knees, pulling him deeper. He hammered into her, giving her what she needed, wanted, had asked him for—a hard, fast, furious fucking.

Drilling deep. Drawing out. Slamming back in, driving her toward another peak, watching her reach it. She throbbed around him. Her expression, the feel of her, dragged him over. Pleasure fisted his balls, then blasted up his spine. Astonishment bit. Gratitude surfaced. Ecstasy stripped him bare, setting his heart in Ferguson's hands, forcing a plea from his throat, exposing him completely as he buried his face in her throat and called her name.

12

On her hands and knees in the middle of the bed, Ferguson thrust back as Kruger powered in, taking her from behind with mind-fuzzing strokes, doing what he'd promised, loving her slow after fucking her hard. The first time he'd taken her blew her mind. The second round nearly killed her. The third was destroying her, pushing her body to the limit while wreaking havoc with her heart.

All part of his plan.

He wanted to love her into oblivion, capture her completely, enslave her with sex while he pummeled her with pleasure. A skilled lover, devoted to the cause, he melded mind and emotion, making her crave him more as he immersed her in delight.

Soft music playing on the speaker across the room. The rough, guttural instructions he murmured and expected her to follow. His long-limbed, hard, strong body holding her in place.

_So._

Effing.

Effective.

Every bit delicious as he made her ride the edge.

Ferguson knew his game, but couldn't locate an

ounce of outrage. No objections here. She wanted him just as much as he did her, adored the way he touched her, reveled in his need for her and the fact he paid attention. To everything. What made her breath hitch, the things that made her shiver, buck, and moan. Learning what she liked and what she didn't. Discovering all her sensitive spots, devastating her with stroke after lazy stroke.

Gripping her hips, Kruger drove deep. Again and again. Over and over. Perfect, rolling ravishment as his hands began to roam.

Tipping her hips, she begged for more without words. His paced stayed steady. A protest caught in the rasp of each breath, abrading the back of her throat. With a murmur, Kruger warned her to stay still, to be a "good girl," *his* good girl, and take him the way he wanted to give it to her.

She moaned into a pillow.

Calloused fingertips swept over her back, along her sides, up her front, from belly to collarbone. He cupped her breasts, wrapping her up, communicating something important. Stubble prickled her skin as he slid her hair out of his way. She felt his teeth then, skimming the top of her shoulder, nipping the side of her neck, sending tingles across her nape. Harsh breaths in her ear. Big hands on her body. Muscled chest pressed to her back. The hot, hard length of him deep inside her.

Heaven.

So unbelievably beautiful.

"You feel it, Fergie?"

Her heart thumped hard behind her breastbone. Words piled up on the tip of her tongue.

"You understand?"

"Yes."

"What am I saying?" he asked, demolishing her with a harder stroke.

Desperation took hold. "*Kruger*."

"Tell me, lass. What am I saying?"

"Mine," she rasped. "Mine."

"Aye, *fazleima*. Every inch of you...*mine*. Precious. You're precious. Sexy as fuck. Smart as hell. Bloody beautiful," he growled. "Love you slow. Fuck you hard. Crack you wide open. Make sure the message gets in, that you believe me."

"I"—her breath hitched—"believe you."

"Nay, you donnae. Not yet, but you will."

"Cowboy—"

"I donnae know what that areshole did tae you. I do feel the pain you carry. Gonna deal with that too." After retreating until she only held the tip of him, Kruger surged back in, driving her higher without upping the pace. "Make you believe."

Hands fisted in the blankets, she whimpered into the sheets.

"What are you tae me?"

Quivering, undone by him, she shook her head.

"What are you?"

"Precious," she whispered, trying to believe, but not knowing how.

No one had ever found her *precious*. Or called her sexy as fuck. Smart as hell she accepted without difficulty. She'd always gotten great grades, received praise for the quickness of her mind from others all her life. What Kruger wanted her to accept was altogether different. An aspect of herself that had been damaged long ago. She'd buried it—her sexuality, the need for physical closeness, the burn for acceptance, her deep desire to give and receive pleasure. All without realizing it.

A coping mechanism. One designed and built by self-protection. A mechanism Kruger had deconstructed with a deliberateness that shocked her.

He was determined, and she was being cracked open, in free fall with no fear of hitting the ground. He would catch her, keep her safe, become her shield anytime she asked him to—anytime he felt it necessary.

He didn't voice the intention. Didn't need to, either. She *felt* it emanating from him, read the resolve, his possessiveness, in the way he touched her, talked to her, in the beat of the connection growing between them. Something supernatural. Something beautiful. Something so intense, it filled her, guiding her out of uncertainty into the fullness of acceptance.

A revelation. One of many since meeting him.

He was so different from what she knew. Completely outside her circle of experience. To be expected in many ways—he was a dragon warrior, a man who didn't care about human convention or propriety. Kruger didn't play by the rules. He took what he wanted without apology. Just like he was taking her now, driving her hard, refusing to let her come, determined to make her *believe*.

Believe she was good enough.

Believe her family was, and had always been, wrong.

Believe he was right, and she was where she'd always belonged.

With word and deed, Kruger pressed the point, obliterating the way she viewed herself, replacing it with the way he saw her. Calling her precious, showing her how much he wanted her, how much he enjoyed looking at her. Telling her she was worthy of his time and attention—that he would never get enough of her. All she needed to do was trust. Trust his intentions. Trust the stark need in his eyes. Trust that he wouldn't betray her the way other men had.

Another brutal thrust. She clenched hard, rippling around him, on the verge, needing to go over. Desperate for him to send her tumbling.

"Again, lass. What are tae me?"

"Precious."

"Aye, you are," he said, firm conviction in his tone. "Now...up."

An incoherent sound left her throat.

He buried himself to the hilt and stayed deep, hips snug against her ass, the insides of his thighs pressed to the outside of hers, holding her still. She was surrounded by him, each movement controlled by him. Rolling his thumb and finger, he tugged on her nipples. The pressure built, drawing her so tight Ferguson knew she was coming apart at the seams.

Ribbons of tension unfurled in her belly. "Oh, God."

"Up on your knees, Ferguson."

His voice curled around her, resonant, deep, gliding over her skin, causing a full-body shiver. Ferguson tried to move. She *needed* to move, take over, get what she needed before he drove her insane.

He stilled her attempt.

A whine escaped her. "Kruger."

His hands separated. One went up to cup her throat, the other slid down, over her the curls between her legs and *in*, hitting her sweet spot. She bucked in his arms. He smiled against her ear and straightened, drawing her up, putting her where he wanted her. Her back settled against his front. His middle finger circled her clit, so gently, teasing her, denying her the firm pressure she needed.

Raising her arms, she grabbed fistfuls of his hair, tipped her chin up, and turned her head. He rewarded her with the wet glide of his tongue over her bottom lip. She pressed her hips into his, begging without words. He kissed her in answer, taking her mouth the way he was loving her—slow and sweet, with brutal intensity.

"What do you say?" Dark eyes glinting in the moonlight streaming through her bedroom windows, he bared his teeth. A sharp nip scored across her bottom lip. "Tell me, lass. What do you say?"

A fast learner, she gave it up without hesitation. "Please."

"There's my good girl. So fucking sweet," he muttered, the rumble coming from deep in his chest as he withdrew, leaving her empty.

"Oh, no. Don't."

"Hold on, baby." Strong hands on her hips, a flex of muscle as he lifted off her knees and turned her. "Want your eyes. Need the green, tae see yer face when you come."

"Effing hell," she rasped.

He laughed. "Wrap me up, Fergie."

She didn't hesitate, wrapping him with her limbs, arms around his shoulders, legs around his waist. Cupping her ass in both hands, he kissed her deep and inched forward on his knees. Her back came up against the headboard. He thrust back inside her, powering up, retreating, coming back, battering her with bliss. She lost his kiss as her spine arched. Long hair flying all over the place, she held on, rolling into each thrust as he began loving her.

Delight sparked down her spine. Tingles took over. She clenched hard, rippling around him, about to go over.

His hand fisted in her hair. "Eyes tae me."

Lips parted on a silent moan, she righted her head. Her gaze collided with his.

"Aye, beauty," he growled, watching pleasure overtake her. "My beauty."

She mewed his name.

"Go, baby. Let me feel you."

Relishing the rough ride, obeying his harsh command, she tumbled off the edge. Ecstasy picked her up, ripped her apart, then put her back together. She heard Kruger's deep rumble as a sharp cry echoed inside the room. His teeth touched her again, drifting over her throat. She bucked. He rode her harder, intensifying the pleasure, giving her more, fingers clenched in her hair, gaze riveted to her face.

She whimpered.

He snarled, driving her down hard before dragging her back up. Once. Twice. A third time before planting himself deep. Dark eyes shimmering, mouth brushing hers, deep voice hitching on her name. Everything about him fit her. Even the roughness of his hands as she gripped his hair, rolled her hips, prolonging his pleasure, hearing him groan, feeling the vibration travel from breast to belly.

"Beauty." Planted deep, muscles twitching, Kruger tucked his face into her throat. A hoarse sound left him. "Beauty. Pure fucking beauty."

"It's you who's beautiful."

His arms tightened around her.

Releasing fistfuls of his hair, she smoothed the thick strands, played a moment, then slid her hands over the tops of his shoulders. Cupping his nape, she hugged him, cradling him as he held her. His mouth moved against her throat. Soft caresses. Profound intimacy. More of Kruger's message conveyed without him saying a word.

Precious.

He found her precious.

Okay. All right.

God, unbelievable. Emotion swelled, tightening her chest. Tears welled as she closed her eyes and touched her lips to his temple. A song stopped playing; another one started. The quiet sound of guitar strings as a woman sang, thanking God for her lover.

Gratitude swelled as she listened to the words. Every bit of the song was true when it came to Kruger. Drawing a shaky breath, Ferguson shivered as he pressed a soft kiss to her pulse point. He flicked her with his tongue, then moved, sitting back on his heels. Arms locked around her, he held her close and rolled. Her back landed on the tangled sheets. He settled on top of her, cupping her ass, his hips between her thighs, still planted deep inside her.

She sucked in a quick breath.

"Sensitive?" he asked, raising his head to look at her.

"Yeah."

"I rode you hard."

"Thank God," she said, echoing the song's sentiment.

"I came three times." Forearm pressed to the bed, he took some of his weight off her and cupped her face. He hummed in contentment, his intense vibe banked but still burning. "Built seven orgasms in you."

"Again, hallelujah."

"My girl likes getting fucked," he said, mischief in his eyes. "No surprise. You're a sweet little piece, McGilvery."

She blinked. "Did you just call me a sweet piece?"

"Aye."

"I'd hit you…if I could lift my arms."

His mouth curved. "I wore you out."

She stifled a yawn. "Mm-hmm."

"Sleepy?"

"Seven orgasms, cowboy," she said, about to lapse into a coma compliments of Kruger's sexual prowess.

"What?" he asked, laugher in his voice. "I let you sleep between rounds two and three."

He had, giving her an hour's rest before rousing her. Fingers stroking featherlight between her legs. Teeth scraping over her throat. Strong thigh pushing hers apart, forcing her knee up and out. A great memory. His touch, the heat in his eyes when she opened hers, was something she'd never forget.

A delicious shiver shook her. "You plan on treating me to a fourth?"

"Aye, but not now," he murmured, brushing his thumb over her lips. "Later. After you get some more sleep. Figure you got three, maybe, four hours before I'll need tae taste you again."

"Seriously?"

"New tae me, lass. Haven't gotten my fill."

"You're a machine."

"Best get used tae it, Fergie. The way you taste, how you like tae fuck, I'm not ever gonna get enough."

"Are you for real?"

"Real as it gets, lass." Dipping his head, he kissed her softly. "Best get used tae that too."

Tendrils of uncertainty crept back in, coiling around her like barbed tentacles. Ferguson felt the cut and slice. She could see the pain coming. The sudden need to run away grabbed hold. Old habits really did die hard. Case in point? Lying beneath Kruger, surrounded by his warmth, aware of his acceptance, and *still*, she wanted to escape. His razor-sharp focus stripped her bare, leaving her nowhere to hide. She needed to backtrack and find safer ground before things went bad. Before she ended up hurt. Again. Like she always did after opening up and trusting.

History didn't lie. The past repeated itself, over and over...and over, again. Nowhere to hide. No place to run. Just the jaws of bad decisions closing around her.

Needing space to collect her thoughts, she pressed her hands to his shoulders and pushed. He didn't budge. She turned her face away. His fingers flexed on her jaw, putting on pressure, bringing her back, refusing to allow her to avoid him.

Battling panic, she squirmed. "Listen—"

"You scared?" Kruger asked, gaze skimming her face.

"Well..." An empty word, nothing but a stalling tactic. A necessary one as the reasons to push him away gathered inside her head. Sorting through the jumbled mess, she stayed silent, working up the courage to be honest, afraid to share too much. A stupid reaction, given she'd just spent the last four hours in bed with him, and Kruger didn't miss much, if anything. Especially when it came to her. "You're a little scary."

"I know."

Her brows popped up. "That's not very reassuring."

"Not gonna lie tae you, Fergie. I'm a dragon warrior who commands immense magic. More powerful than most of my kind. I *am* scary. Should be too, tae everyone but you," he said, doing what he always did, giving it to her straight. "Natural for you tae have doubts. Be a little unsure. New place. New people. The emergence of yer magic and true calling. You wanna protect yerself. Like I said, natural, baby. I'm new tae you too, and we didnae start out in the best way."

The understatement of the year. Still...

"Straight up, I acted like an arsehole. No excuse for it, except seeing you for the first time...shite, lass. Strong. Spirited. Energy sparking all over the place. So fucking beautiful, I lost my wits for a while. I insulted you, threatened you, yelled at you, instead of doing what I should've the second I saw you."

"What?"

"Got you naked and fucked you on your desk."

Her eyes widened. "Fucked me on my desk?"

"Mm-hmm. I'm thinking that's my next move."

"Kruger—"

"I insulted you, baby, put pain in yer eyes. Never gonna forgive myself for that."

Tears tickled the back of her throat. Ignoring the itch, she stopped trying to push him away. She hadn't expected him to bring it up. God, an apology. A weird one, but with Kruger she'd take what she could get. "Good thing for you I'm more of a peacemaker. I don't hold grudges."

"Something else we need tae work on."

"What's that supposed to mean?"

"Fergie, I said some bad shite, hurt yer feelings, and instead of scorching me where I stood, you offered me a scotch."

Scorching him where he stood?

Seriously?

"I don't know how to do that yet."

"Lucky for me. Otherwise, I'd be little more than a dark stain on yer carpet," he said, smiling as she laughed. "But my point stands. You're the innkeeper. You donnae take shite from anyone. Me included. If someone gets in yer face, you hammer him first, ask questions later. Leave the scotch in the fucking cabinet."

Wonder crept in. She stared at him, struggling to wrap her brain around his awesomeness.

He grew impatient. "We clear?"

"Kind of," she whispered.

"What needs clearing up?"

"I'm just... Everything's... It's a lot, Kruger. The Parkland, the guests, the inn talking to me, the way I feel about you. It's happening too fast...so fast, it's confusing."

"I know that too. But I'm patient, and you've got time, Fergie. Time tae settle in, tae sort yer head and come tae terms. Though best you understand now, yer confusion willnae keep me out of yer bed." He flexed his hips, nudging sensitive places. Pleasure burned through her. Her breath caught as she tightened around him. "I'm planted deep in more ways than one. I need you. I want you. I'm not going anywhere."

"Kruger?"

"Right here, lass."

"I can just say..."

"What?"

"You can talk to me too, you know?"

"About what?"

"Whatever's bothering you," she said, hesitating, unsure whether she should bring it up, but avoidance never made for a good game plan.

Still, cornering Kruger was a crapshoot, one not many would survive, but she couldn't let it stand. She might be confused, but he was hurting, worried, hiding in plain sight. Maintaining a mirage instead of letting his true self shine through.

She felt the weight of it, sensed the burden he carried without being told it was there. The bond she shared with him clued her in. No details included, but...man, it was heavy. So effing heavy. Weighing him down, causing deep anxiety to invade the energy humming around him, and her antennae to twitch, making it impossible for him to hide from her.

"I've got you in my arms," he murmured. "Nothing's bothering me, lass."

"Don't lie to me, Kruger."

"I'm not—"

"You're keeping a secret. A big one."

His big frame tensed. Heavy muscles rippled, pressing into her as unease entered his eyes, making already dark shift to pitch black. "Fergie—"

"We're connected now, you and I."

"Aye."

"You wanted me to feel it, and I do."

"I feel you too, lass."

"Then you gotta know you're not fooling me. I sense it. Hidden away, buried deep, like a thorn in your paw. It's bothering you...worrying you, killing you a little at a time," she said, fighting to keep her tone even in the face of his growing ferocity. He owned a temper, an explosive one—she'd witnessed its nastiness firsthand. Hopefully, she wouldn't see it again...at least, not directed at her. "I'm guessing it has something to do with why you want The White Hare. You think buying it will solve your problem, but—"

"Lass—"

"—it won't."

"Fuck."

"It won't, Kruger," she said, hooking her knee higher around his hip. Calf nestled against the small of his back, she set her hands on his chest and gave him a gentle shove. He rolled onto his back. She quiv-

ered as he slid out of her, but stayed on task and settled astride him. "Don't get me wrong, I'm not
pushing. The secret's yours to keep or share. I just
wanted you to know I know, and...I'm here when
you're ready."

His hands flexed on her hips. "Jesus, lass."

"Whatever's going on," she whispered, "you can
talk to me. We'll figure it out together."

Brow furrowed, he looked away. A muscle twitched
in his jaw.

Lifting her hand, she smoothed the twitch with
her fingertips. "It's going to be okay."

"You psychic now?"

"No idea." She could be—not much of a stretch,
given all the changes she was experiencing. She already saw ghosts. Maybe clairvoyance came part and
parcel with running an inn full of supernatural creatures with violent tendencies and few scruples.
"Maybe that's what I'm turning out to be. Might come
in handy if the pride of werelions on the third floor
decide to eat somebody. Cut them off at the pass."

"Fucking hell," he growled, amusement creeping
into his tone.

"I'm guessing one of the water nymphs." She kept
going, letting the heavier topic slide in favor of lightening the mood. "Or Ascot."

"Who's Ascot?"

"The concierge."

"The giant rat?"

"Chinchilla, actually, but yeah."

"No one would miss him," Kruger muttered, gathering her long hair in his hand.

"Hendrix might."

"Doubtful."

She grinned at him.

Fingers playing in the bright red strands, Kruger tugged at her scalp, then cupped the nape of her neck. He drew her down, tucking her head beneath his chin, her cheek against his chest, then reached out. Grabbing the corner of the comforter, he yanked the covers over them. "No more talking. Time for sleep."

"Cowboy—"

"Sleep, *fazleima*."

Ferguson hesitated, trying to decide. Let him get away with avoiding the issue? Or dig for answers with the aim of extracting the thorn from his paw? She debated a moment, then let it go. For now. She'd said what she needed to say. He hadn't liked it, but she knew he'd heard her. Pressing him right now wouldn't land him—or her—anywhere good. Tomorrow would be soon enough to dig deep, open old wounds, and heal the hurt.

With a wiggle, she closed her eyes and snuggled in. "`Night, Kruger."

"Sweet dreams, lass."

Two days ago, she would've sworn getting a good night's sleep was unlikely, and *sweet dreams* an impossibility. But surrounded by Kruger's heat, with his hands on her body, Ferguson had a feeling she'd sleep like a baby.

At least for tonight. Tomorrow would be another story, bringing new challenges and frustrations...along with crushing defeats. Experience was a good lesson, and she was an excellent student. The future was unpredictable, which meant she must live in the now, enjoy every second of being in Kruger's arms before life threw her another curveball and things took a turn for the worse.

13

F lat on his back with Ferguson sprawled on top of him, Kruger stared up at the ceiling, the scent of cinnamon and sex in the air...along with a healthy amount of panic.

He could feel it circling just below the surface. The bubble and burn in his veins. The grind of unease in his heart. The overwhelming urge to run far and get there fast.

Battling the impulse, he breathed around the lump sitting like a stone in the center of his chest. Straight up, he was an arsehole, the lowest of the low for giving Ferguson the wrong impression—for encouraging her, for calling her precious, for pushing his claim and telling her he planned to stay.

He clenched his teeth. "Bloody hell."

He was an arsehole.

Shame burned through him as he replayed his conversation with her. Guilt joined the stampeding parade trampling his good sense. Goddess strike him dead—he'd made her say it out loud, even forced her to repeat his words, so caught up in the moment he'd wanted nothing more than for her to view herself the way he saw her: strong, smart, spirited. Worthy of the best life had to offer.

That was little more than an hour ago. Despite the chaotic twist inside his head, nothing had changed.

He stood by every word. But with quiet descending, doubt closed ranks, making him question his ability to keep her, to provide what she needed and make her happy—for more than just one night. Giving and receiving pleasure was one thing; claiming Ferguson for his own was quite another. Mating a female took time, attention, and shitloads of energy. All-out commitment. The kind he'd never wanted to make, and...

Goddamn it.

How in the hell had he allowed this to happen?

He knew better than to get involved. To take a female he couldn't leave behind without a backward glance. Everyone he fucked knew the drill. He never minced words or hid his intentions. Brutal honesty. Mutual agreement of the rules upfront. Zero chance of a second visit. Nothing but an hour or two of pleasure and the understanding he would never stay.

He wanted to kill Wallaig. The bastard had given him bad advice.

Touching Ferguson had been a mistake. A huge one, given what happened in the aftermath: a deep connection, soul-searing acceptance, a bond so strong he could no longer do what needed to be done—get up, get out of her flat, and get on with his plan for The White Hare. As fast as fucking possible.

Dread hammered him like a mailed fist.

Kruger flinched. His arms flexed around Ferguson. Attuned to him even in sleep, she reacted to his turmoil, shifting, whispering his name, sweeping her hand across his bare chest, a light touch meant to soothe him. He closed his eyes. Goddess forgive him. She deserved better. Deserved more than he was, or had to offer. And yet he didn't move away. He stayed where he was—planted in her bed, holding her close as he murmured to reassure her.

The sound of his voice settled her.

Satisfaction rumbled through him.

He cursed the manner of his birth, his own name along with his violent nature. He wasn't an honorable male. He knew that, had never claimed to be anything other than he was—a corporate raider, a cold-blooded warrior without mercy or conscience. Somehow, though, Ferguson made him want to be more. A good male instead of one tainted by self-interest and ruthless intent.

Too much to ask? He scowled at the tongue-and-groove planks overhead. Probably. Ninety-five percent likely, if he allowed himself to think about it too long. Which meant he needed to go. Right now. Before she woke up armed with expectations.

Self-preservation screamed, *Go! Get out before it's too late.*

His body refused to heed the warning, forcing him to stay when all he wanted to do was go. Rolling out of bed, slipping away, taking to open skies was the right thing to do—the only way forward before he lost his mind, did the unthinkable, and took more. Got in too deep and accepted what she offered—sanctuary, a place for him to belong, everything he wanted but knew he didn't deserve and could never have, but...

She smelled good, and felt even better pressed up against him. A stark slice of paradise with her gorgeous curves, candy cane scent, and petal-soft skin.

Fucking energy-fuse.

He'd always thought the bond between mates was

a good thing, the be-all and end-all for a Dragonkind warrior, the missing link a male searched for his entire life. His brothers-in-arms provided excellent examples. All his packmates yearned for a female, someone to claim and call his own. For his perfect match— body, heart, mind, and bioenergy. To be well fed every night, loved every day, and accepted despite his short-comings.

Most Dragonkind felt the same way.

Why, then, did the idea make him sick to his stom-ach? The pitch and roll threw him off balance, bashing him against mental rocks, drowning him in uncertainty, making it hard to breathe. Stay or go. The pleasure of holding her versus the pain of leaving her behind. Two sides of the same coin, now working like allied forces inside him, pushing, pulling, dragging him one way only to shove him in the opposite di-rection.

The seesaw made him want to break things. And yet, like a child with his favorite toy, he cradled Fergu-son, holding on tight, listening to her breathe, watching over her while she slept but trying to talk himself into letting her go.

No word of a lie, he was going to kill Wallaig.

His friend should've known better. The male was mated, for fuck's sake, was well versed in the power of energy-fuse and what it meant for a Dragonkind war-rior. Wallaig had sent him headlong into danger any-way, landing him in the middle of a battle he didn't know how to fight. Now, he was stuck, mired in an emotional wasteland, so far from his normal mental state his mind fogged.

Goodbye, comfort zone; hello, confusion.

The second he touched Ferguson, the lines had blurred. She became his sole focus. Her comfort was his greatest wish—her needs, his fixation. Her well-being jumped to the top of his list, becoming all-important as his dragon locked on, accepting her as the one made for him.

The way she affected him blew past boundaries.

Watching his brothers react to their chosen females should've clued him in. He'd chosen to embrace obliviousness instead, watching without truly *seeing*. Now, he stood neck-deep in trouble, struggling to comprehend how it happened while trying to negotiate with nature and find a way out.

Out of wanting her. Out of needing her. Out of disappointing her if his better angels won, and he managed to leave her hale and whole, untarnished by the likes of him and the memories they might've made together. One night was enough. It would have to be enough, but...

Having had her—touched her, loved her—Kruger didn't know if he was strong enough to let her go. He knew what she felt like in his arms, how she sounded when she came, still had the taste of her on his tongue. He'd fallen hard, way too fast, becoming enthralled by her. Her temper. Her intelligence. The spirit she showed when she went head to head with him. Ferguson gave as good as she got, challenging him, sparring with him, obeying his commands in bed with such joy he couldn't believe his good fortune.

She was passionate, forthright, bold, and beautiful. The four pillars males searched for in a female, but rarely found.

Hugging her closer, Kruger breathed deep. His chest expanded, drawing the scent of her into his lungs. Contentment stole through him. His dragon purred, soothed and settled for once, instead of wild and restless. Being well fed by the brilliance of Ferguson's bioenergy was part of it. Being well fucked, riding the buzz of sexual satisfaction, was another. His emotional ties with her, though, took a bigger piece of the pie, leaving him so relaxed he slid into repletion against his will.

A dangerous drift, given he already knew he wasn't built for connection. His history proved it. No matter how much he wanted to, he couldn't ignore the evidence.

A lifetime of file folders filled with damning proof piled up inside his head. As he flipped through the pages, his thoughts spiraled, pointing to an unavoidable conclusion: pursuing a relationship with Ferguson was folly. It would end badly. For him, sure. But mostly for her. Claiming her in the way of his kind wasn't a good idea. No matter how well intentioned, tying her to him would hurt her in the end.

The realization caused icy needles to poke into his skin. He laid out all the reasons he must roll out of her bed and never return.

The filth running through his veins sat at the top. His sire hadn't left him much: abandonment, disdain, betrayal. Nothing good sat on the branches of his family tree. His true origin turned the sliver of hope he clung to into disillusionment. Ugliness crept in from the edges, painting his insides with a filthy brush. It always did when he thought about Silfer—and what the Dragon God had done. The male's legacy tainted his son's, making Kruger feel dirty.

And worse, Ferguson had asked him about it.

Spirit bright with honesty, she'd invited him to share, handed him the perfect opening—tempted him with the idea that she might be able to wash him clean, wipe away the filth he lived with every night and each day. His mate knew he was hiding something. Something huge. Something so big, she'd read the shame in his eyes, and no doubt seen the slime smeared on his soul.

Hell, she'd gone a step further—guessing the reason he'd targeted The White Hare in the first place.

Smart. His girl was so bloody sharp.

Without effort, she boiled the situation down to its basic elements, picking through the threads, tugging at the most sensitive stings, urging him to tell her the truth when he knew it would be the end of him. The end of her too, if he wasn't careful, and—

"Kruger?"

Her sleepy voice swarmed his senses. Pleasure buzzed down his spine.

Kruger exhaled and reached for calm. "Shh."

"Whaz—"

"Nothing, *fazleima*."

"You—"

"Go back tae sleep, lass. It's all good."

"Uh-oh," she mumbled, one-quarter awake, three-quarters asleep.

His lips twitched. "What?"

"Big thoughts."

"Nay, baby. I'm just—"

"Tell me."

"Fergie—"

"Can't sleep," she said, slurring her words while hitting the nail on the head. He couldn't sleep, didn't want to close his eyes and miss a moment of holding her when he might never get another chance. "Tell me."

"Later."

Her eyelashes fluttered, sweeping his skin. "Lying."

Kruger huffed. "Smart lass."

"Cowboy—"

"Tomorrow," he whispered, knowing she was right. He was lying. He'd been doing it his entire life. To his brothers-in-arms. To himself. And now, to his mate. "We'll talk tomorrow."

"Promise?"

"Aye," he said, not meaning it. No way in hell would he tell her. Secrets got out that way. Once one person knew, anything could happen. There'd be absolute hell to pay if Cyprus and his brothers-in-arms found out what he'd worked so hard to hide. "Let me enjoy having you in my arms."

"Gorgeous."

"Aye, you are."

She hummed. "No, you are—beautiful... so beautiful."

His chest tightened. "Fuck, Fergie."

"You feel good, Kruger."

His throat went tight. "Bonnie lass, you undo me."

"Finally." Her mouth brushed his skin. He closed his eyes as she pressed a kiss over his heart. "Getting somewhere."

"Mm-hmm," he murmured, drawing circles on her lower back with his fingertips.

She sighed.

He kept up the gentle touches, stroking his hands over her. Softly. Sweetly. Drinking her in, memorizing the feel of her, encouraging her to go back to sleep. Little by little, she sank back beneath the wave, into deep slumber. He relaxed along with her, but continued caressing her. His hands swept over her skin. His hum of enjoyment turned into a low rumble.

He should stop, let her sleep, maybe even join her. He veered off course instead and, cupping the back of her thigh, rolled onto his side. Her eyelashes flickered as she hooked her leg over his hip and snuggled closer. He pressed a kiss to her temple, watched her settle, then turned his nose into her hair. She smelled fantastic, like evergreens, candy canes, sex...and him.

An alluring combination.

He breathed her in, questioning his intentions along with his sanity. One circuit turned into two, three, then more as he stroked up her back, down her side and over her hip. Gorgeous curves pressed along his length, the beauty of her all around him. Unable to stop, he caressed her gently and time passed, pushing the clock toward two a.m.

Prime fighting time.

A fact he couldn't miss as Wallaig knocked on his cerebral door. *Knock, knock, knock,* came every few minutes, making it difficult for him to ignore the persistent SOB rapping on his temples. His XO wanted a word. Not needing to hear "I told you so," he centered his attention on Ferguson, refusing to give his friend any headspace, ignoring the demand he open a connection into mind-speak.

The knock turned into battering ram.

He winced. With a low growl, Kruger flipped the switch. *"What?"*

"You barking at me?"

"I'm gonna do more than that when I see you."

"Any idea when that'll be?"

Kruger snapped his teeth together. The sharp click echoed through mind-speak.

"Not done with her yet?"

Unable to pry his molars apart, he stayed silent.

Wallaig snorted. *"I'll take that as a nay."*

"Take it however you want."

"Aye, laddie. Nowhere near done," Wallaig said,

sounding amused. *"Gonna fuck her again? Should I tell Cyprus tae—"*

"Bugger off, mon."

"I want tae say I told you so, but—"

"I'll rip yer tail off and shove it up yer arse, if you do."

Wallaig chuckled.

Kruger bit back a curse, trying to control his temper. *"Where are you?"*

"Airborne. We've got movement."

"Grizgunn?"

"Aye."

"Where?"

"South," Wallaig said. *"I'm tracking a shite-load of trace energy. Two full fighting triangles. The bastard's heading toward Edinburgh."*

"Outside the three-mile marker?"

"Aye. Cloaked and keeping a good distance. We donnae want him tae know we're here. At least, not yet."

"See what he's up tae."

"That's the plan." The sound of rising wind howled through the link. Scales rattled as Wallaig shifted course. *"Got Levin and Ran with me. Cyprus, Tydrin, Vyroth, and Tempel are hugging the coastline, keeping an eye out."*

Kruger grunted. Not a bad plan, though, it was a hunt he needed to join. If he didn't, his packmates would have all the fun and he'd end up—

"You gonna roll outta bed and join us?"

"Aye." He set his mouth against the crown of Ferguson's head. *"Give me a minute or two. Five tops, and I'll be—"*

Magic sliced into the room.

Ferguson jolted against him. Her head came up. Her eyes opened. Her gaze fired, moving from normal green to emerald shimmer as she shoved up and away from him. The veil of sleep around her ripped open as she landed on her knees, bouncing on the mattress beside him.

"What the fuck?"

"Shit!" she said.

Frozen in place, he felt her focus sharpen. Starlight rolled overhead, flickering like an array of fairy lights. A tremor rumbled through the room. The lamps sitting on the bedside table rattled. He reached for her. Naked, pale skin dusted by the faint glow, she avoided his hand and swiveled on her knees, attention snapping to the bank of wide windows opposite the bed.

"Fergie—"

A low growl left her throat.

His mouth fell open.

"Move!"

"Lass, what—"

"Now!" Grabbing his wrist, she yanked him toward the side of the bed. "Intruders. There are—"

Boom!

The explosion slammed into the side of the building. The wall rocked. Shattering glass blew inward. Foundation stones crumbled, throwing shrapnel as a fireball exploded into the room. The smell of gasoline ate through clean air. Heat licked over his skin. He heard Wallaig yell through mind-speak a second before the shock wave struck. The bed flipped up and over, rolling end over end, sending him flying as wood splintered, and Ferguson gasped in pain.

14

B reathing in smoke, Grizgunn sliced through the layer of smog floating over Edinburgh. The noxious scent burned over his senses, seeping into his mouth and down his throat. He breathed deep. His mouth curved, baring the tips of his fangs. The toxic fog tasted good and felt even better, coating his acid-blue scales, sticking to the webbing of his wings like radioactive sludge, making him glow in the dark.

Particles of heating oil sparked against the tip of his tail. The muted flash-bangs made him grin.

He didn't like humans, couldn't abide close contact without wanting to slice one's throat, but the environmental wasteland the assholes left in their wake was brilliant. The absolute best. A downward spiral beaten out to the rhythm of *mess, mess, more beautiful, intoxicating mess.*

Most Dragonkind hated the pollution. His venomous half reveled in it, soaring through poisonous clouds, drinking in the toxicity. The environmental movement should thank him, erect monuments to his prowess, give him a plaque that said Number One Poison-Eater for sucking in the foul brume and spitting out clean air. A living filter for their never-ending filth.

One of a kind in their world...and also in the one he occupied. A fact the warriors he flew toward would learn tonight.

Wings spread wide, he banked into a wide turn. The foul brume thickened, enclosing him in a pocket of nastiness that blurred streetlights powered by LEDs below him.

Hidden deep inside a cloaking spell, he jetted over the suburbs toward the city center. A cache of neoclassical buildings hollowed out into parks, then ramped into neighborhoods. Apartment complexes spiked upward, interrupting the flow, forcing townhouses with small back gardens into clusters sandwiched between narrow streets and wider thoroughfares. All lit up in the hopes of scaring the dreaded bogeyman away.

Grizgunn huffed. Fat chance of that happening. What humans didn't know would eventually kill them.

He hadn't realized it at first, but Scotland breathed in magic and spat out myth. Whispered stories abounded in taverns and small towns—strange happenings, odd disappearances, none of it human-driven—telling him Dragonkind wasn't the only magical species to inhabit the Highlands.

Odd in lots of ways.

Denmark, his home for over fifty years, wasn't like Scotland. He'd never felt the presences of *others*. Evidence of different tribes littered the ground and polluted the air here, invading the brume, spiraling across his senses—making him want to hunt and kill, to annihilate and cause a slew of extinctions.

A snarl rumbled up his throat. His muscles tensed as his dragon half vibrated with aggression.

Grizgunn locked it down, forcing his beast to wash the taint of the others' magic away and stay on task.

His eyes narrowed on the financial district. Historical landmarks, statues, and old churches dotted the shifting terrain. All spotlit in the dark, shining like a beacon for visitors and tourists, showing the cash cows off to maximum effect.

He huffed in disgust. Human cities—the equivalent of silver platter, providing an endless supply of hot spots to target and destroy.

His gaze narrowed on a cathedral as he wondered how it would feel to let go, to lean into his inclination and lay waste to Edinburgh, instead of quelling the urge. One exhale, little more than a blip on his magical scale, and entire neighborhoods would be engulfed in bilious green fire. Total destruction followed by the predictable hue and cry. The usual idiocy as thousands of humans asked stupid questions—*what, why, and how*?

Tempting. He flexed his talons. Oh so very tempting, but...

Maybe another time, when he wasn't eyeballs-deep in a mission.

Swinging into a wide turn, he sliced over a park with a huge putting green at its center. Storefronts planted along wide sidewalks surrounded the green space humans no doubt strolled inside during the day. Right now, though, it was empty. No one in sight. Nothing but tall trees standing alone, leaves rustling in the breeze as he flew overhead and set up his final approach.

Edinburgh Castle dead ahead. The Royal Mile beyond it, acting like a runway into Holyroodhouse.

Five minutes tops, and he'd land in the palace garden. The males he planned to meet were already there. He sensed the trio waiting, standing in the woods behind the main building. Turning a mental dial, he adjusted his sonar. A ping sounded inside his head. His eyes narrowed as he gauged the distance to his target. Four miles out. Three unknown warriors on his radar, a tight-knit group. Powerful trace energy frothing around each one. A positive sign...if things went his way.

Contrails kicking off his wingtips, Grizgunn blasted over the wide, cobbled expanse of the Royal Mile. A straight shot from Castle Crag. Less than a minute until touch down. Time to set it up. He opened a link into mind-speak.

The connection boomeranged and came back around, collecting his warriors along the way. He waited for each to link in, then growled. *"Sitrep."*

"In position," Ingolf said, Danish accent deepening with excitement.

An understandable reaction. After months of playing keep-away with the Scottish pack, Ingolf wanted to kill something. The circumstances under which that happened didn't matter to the male, just as long as he got his claws bloody. Grizgunn applauded the initiative, but planned to disappoint his warrior tonight. He needed the trio alive, as allies, not rivals. Building a stronger pack to fight the Scots was impera- tive. He didn't need his warriors going off script and killing potential recruits before he assessed their wor- thiness.

"South side?" he asked, adjusting his radar.

"Ja, I'm perched on top of the tallest building. Bjorn's posted up on the east side, and—"

"I'm settled into my blind on the west," Steiner said, tone so low Grizgunn could hardly hear him. *"I want to go in, be with you when you meet them."*

Of course he did. As a stone dragon, Steiner lived up to his name. He was a brute, so short-tempered anger pulled his strings, making him difficult to control.

"Stay where you are," Grizgunn said, denying Steiner's request. *"Hakon and I will handle it."*

Flying off his right wingtip, Hakon bumped him with the side of his tail.

Pain prickled over Grizgunn's flank. He scowled at his XO. His friend grinned, flashing huge fangs. Muttering a curse under his breath, Grizgunn returned his attention to the setup. *"Full scan, boys. No one waiting in the weeds?"*

"I'm roaming, playing sweeper five miles out," Ezpen said, scales rattling through the connection. *"Sky's clear. Radar's clean in every direction."*

"Good." Grizgunn scanned the sky one more time. *"Making my final approach. Keep it tight. Stay alert. If the trio turns out to be unfriendly—"*

"Please, goddess, let it be so," Steiner muttered. *"I haven't gotten my claws bloody in months."*

Ingolf growled in agreement.

Per usual, Bjorn said nothing, but Grizgunn felt the weight of the male's hope, his need for combat, from miles away.

"Can't say I disagree," Hakon said, throwing him a sidelong look. One that said, *Pretty please with whipped cream and a cherry on top.*

"Fuck," he mumbled, unease pricking along his spine.

Something didn't feel right. The wild scent on the breeze, maybe. The charge in the air, perhaps. Grizgunn didn't know what bothered him. He couldn't place the feeling, never mind nail it down. The setup seemed sound. All the boxes had been ticked, and yet he couldn't sideline the idea something bad waited in the wings.

He never should've sent Tigmar and Ansgar to surveil The White Hare. Not tonight. The meeting with the trio behind Holyrood House was important, potentially life-changing. It was, and should be, the priority. But with Tigmar in a tizzy about financial records, inconsistent business practices, and the Scottish pack's possible involvement, Grizgunn had been left with two options: send Tigmar north to investigate the property with backup to watch his six, or strangle the male and sprinkle his ashes over the crag. He'd picked the lesser of two evils, allowing his warrior to keep on breathing.

Tigmar had been ecstatic with the assignment. Steiner had looked like he wanted to rip his own horns off. Hakon had approved of Grizgunn's restraint, trying not to laugh at the stupidity of the situation.

Speed steady, guard up, Grizgunn spiraled over Holyroodhouse, then banked into a fast turn. Muscles along his side stretched. Pain rippled over his shoulders. A tension headache pierced his temples as he spun into another rotation, letting the warriors on the ground sense his arrival. Hidden in the trees, the trio shifted. Powerful magic rippled out in concentric circles, sparking across his scales, pushing against the limits of his own.

"Jesus," he murmured, rocketing across the treetops toward open ground.

"Told you." Steady on his wingtip, Hakon cut through the snarl, flicking off the other warriors' magic. *"Powerful sons of bitches."*

Another round of unease hit Grizgunn. The trio didn't make sense: three males, all skilled fighters. No need for them to join an already established group. Warriors who wielded the kind of power he perceived could draw other Dragonkind to whatever sector they chose and start their own pack. Which raised an important question—why in the hell were the males in Scotland?

Instinct warned him alternative motives were afoot. He should turn around and fly away. Now, before things went from slightly off to totally fucked up. He didn't need the added risk or headache, but...

He clenched his teeth.

The warriors below presented a unique opportunity. If the males really were homeless, he could sway them, turn them—forge them into a fighting unit so lethal, Cyprus wouldn't know what hit him. A big risk with a serious upside, one Grizgunn refused to let pass him by. Despite the danger, he was curious now. The urge to solve the riddle—to smooth out the inconsistencies—pushed him forward...into the unsafe territory with the potential of a huge reward.

Not smart, but...

Six against three were good odds. Whatever the trio's motives, he had enough firepower at his back to discourage a direct attack.

Rocketing over the residential area backing onto a manicured lawn, he put on the brakes. The dark blue webbing vibrated as he cleared the thick fringe of huge trees. He folded his wings. Gravity yanked him toward the ground. Damp air whistled over his scales. His paws slammed down. He turned toward a sprawling oak, sharp claws cutting through the top layer of turf. The smell of loam and fresh-cut grass sliced up, tickling his nostrils as he leveled his gaze on the males standing deep in shadows.

Three pairs of eyes were on him. One the blue-gray of the north Atlantic, the second the color of ice, the last a flat, shimmering silver.

Already in human form, the largest male stepped from the shadows.

Grizgunn swallowed a curse. Yes. Absolutely. Fucking powerful. Tall, six foot eight, maybe six foot nine, with a huge frame. Thin twin scars marked a face set in an intense expression. His shoulders were squared as though prepared for a fight. The lethal vibe ate through the gloom around him. A leader who understood his own strength. A commander who demanded the kind of respect Grizgunn refused to give anyone.

Shit.

It was all going to *shit*.

One look, and Grizgunn knew he didn't want this male anywhere near his warriors. He would try to oust him as commander of the Danish pack. It was simply a part of his nature. Easy to read in the line of his—

"Grizgunn?" Feet planted beneath stout branches overhead, the male crossed his arms over his chest.

Shifting out of dragon form, Grizgunn conjured his clothes. "*Ja*. And you are?"

"Callas." With a flick of his fingers, the male indicated the others standing behind him. "My wingmates —Beauregard and Rune."

A weird accent, difficult for Grizgunn to place. Greek, maybe. Or—his eyes narrowed—Northern Africa, perhaps. With undertones of British colonialism.

He raised a brow. "You're a long way from home."

Callas shrugged. "Needed a change of scenery."

"And you found it here?"

"Depends."

"On what?"

"Who you've got in your stable, and whether or not we get along."

Smart. Careful. Callas was both, and yet Grizgunn didn't like the feel of him. The male talked a good line, but smelled all wrong.

"You looking to own?" he asked, testing Callas's boundaries, trying to unearth his intentions.

"I'm looking to settle."

Settle, his ass. The male hadn't flown into Scotland to put down roots. Callas was after something. Or—Grizgunn's instinct clanged—perhaps someone. "You don't have the look and feel of a settler."

"Not gonna lie," Callas said, rolling his shoulders. "I've led a pack. Been there, done that. Got my brothers-in-arms out of it. Don't feel the need to repeat the experience. And I like the feel of this island."

"Enough water for you."

"Mountains and streams, too."

"Best of both worlds for a water dragon."

Callas inclined his head, answering without really confirming. No need to put a finer point on it—the strong smell of brine in his scent gave him away. Staring at him, Grizgunn took a moment to marvel at the male. Water dragons were rare. Aggressive, unpredictable—and completely untrustworthy.

By all accounts, Callas's subset of Dragonkind was fickle, loyal to no one but themselves. Self-interest always won out in the end. Which made Callas a terrible gamble. The males standing at the water dragon's back might refute his assertion, but Grizgunn didn't care. Less than five minutes, a couple of words exchanged, and he knew deep down Callas and his wingmates needed to fly away.

Now. Before dawn crested the horizon.

The sooner the trio moved on—to Ireland, maybe, given Callas's affinity for islands—the better for the Danish pack. Allowing the trio to stay in his territory was a bad idea. One that would no doubt get him killed and the warriors he commanded—

"Shit," Callas growled, glancing skyward. "Please, tell me that's one of yours."

Grizgunn frowned. "What—"

Shock waves rippled over the lawn. Hurricane winds slammed into the treetops. Branches splintered. Shrapnel cut across his skin. Blood running down his face, Grizgunn snarled a command through mind-speak, warning his warriors as the ground rumbled beneath his feet. The turf cracked open. A dark brown dragon erupted from the earth, launching dirt sky high.

Glowing green eyes narrowed on Grizgunn. The enemy dragon bared his fangs and exhaled hard.

Rock bullets the size of his fist machine-gunned over the grass.

"Earth dragon!" Callas shouted, smooth blue scales flashing as he tried to get out of range. "Beau, Rune—get airborne!"

His friends grunted, shifted, and shot skyward.

Already in dragon form, Grizgunn pressed his wings to his flank and torqued into a spine-bending spiral. Hakon rocketed into open air, taking a swipe at the enemy dragon on the flyby. The lethal barrage of sharp stones slammed into the ground beneath him. Rock and loam sprayed across his scales. The smell of dirty gasoline ripped through clear air. He unfolded his wings and burst out of the clearing. As he blasted over Holyroodhouse, he searched for his warriors in the fray. In full flight, his pack closed ranks, trying to get to him, cutting off the Scots' attack and—

Boom!

Lightning forked overhead. A fireball split the sky, cutting through the gloom.

The burning stream of muck struck the circular driveway below him. The ground cratered. Treetops caught fire. The fountain exploded, throwing stone and water across the palace's façade. Windows shattered. The concussive shock wave hurled Grizgunn sideways. Molten lava spewed upward, arching through the dark.

Caught in the crossfire, Callas roared in pain.

Grizgunn hissed as the fire-acid splattered across his scales. His claws started to smoke as the poison went to work, eating through his interlocking dragon skin. Pain fed his fury. Aggression made him rise.

With a snarl, he gained altitude, then banked, swinging one way, then the other. His wings sawed, changing his trajectory mid-flight, moving with the blast instead of against it.

Might as well make it interesting.

Cyprus thought he could ambush him and win. Grizgunn knew better. The enemy had just injured Callas, pissing off a water dragon along with his brothers-in-arms. Never a good idea. He might not like the trio, but add the males to his own warriors already poised to strike and...*ja*. His pack held the advantage, even if the commander of the Scottish pack, the whoreson responsible for stealing his birthright, didn't yet know it.

15

The explosion rocked the room.

Made of solid stone, the outer wall blew inward. Windows shattered as the blast picked up the heavy bedframe, flipping it end over end. Wood cracked. Shock splintered reality as the mattress heaved and Ferguson flew, tumbling over the footboard. The boom was deafening. Debris nicked her skin, flying like shrapnel.

She didn't have time to scream—or react—before the shock wave hit.

Kruger reacted for her. Using his body to shield her, he wrapped himself around her. She curled her limbs around him, spinning in midair. Completely out of control, he tumbled along with her.

Pressed tight to his strong frame, she tucked her head beneath his chin and hung on hard. He growled. The low sound reverberated through his chest into hers. The air thickened. The room whirled. Fire licked overhead, orange waves crackling against the planked ceiling.

Kruger contracted around her. She let him, mind frenzied, body plummeting as an indescribable force rippled around him and captured her. One second spun into the next. The odd vibration emanating from Kruger intensified, making her skin tingle and realization strike.

Magic. What she was feeling was *magic*. Burning hot and hard all around him.

If she'd been thinking clearly, she would've realized sooner. She'd never seen him shift, but knew he was part dragon. The powerful current was his magic firing, expanding, contracting, weaving a spell, creating a bubble of protection. Fine as spider silk, a glowing green web formed around them. Whirling debris slammed against the barrier, then sliced through the half-formed shield, clawing over her shoulder.

She smelled the blood. Felt the pain. Heard Kruger curse, and...

Agony turned into self-preservation. Her mind expanded. Her perception shifted. An unseen seam opened inside her. Something fierce slipped its leash, rising to greet the moment.

The force blasted through the breach. Electric current raced down her spine. The fine hairs on her nape stood on end. Kruger flinched, reacting to the shift in the air, arms tensing around her.

Another jolt hit her.

She jerked, nausea driving bile up her throat as sparks arced from her fingertips. The sharp shards raked her palms, flickered, died, then throbbed to life again. The creases on her hands began to glow. Power gathered, streaming up her arms as she and Kruger stopped going up and began to come down.

Debris scraped against the webbing.

Unable to make sense of the internal shift, she stared at her hands, feeling the force inside her expand and gain speed. White light turned into a bright green glow against her skin. Instinct whispered.

Knowledge she didn't own—and had never learned—
pierced her mind. Images flashed across her mental
screen, giving her direction, demanding she protect
the inn and stop the assault.

"Fergie—"

Another blast detonated, rocking her room, cutting off his voice.

Busted furniture flew, bashing into the bookcase.
The inferno roared. Smoke billowed up. The sphere—
strong as steel, light as air—slammed into wooden
floorboards, then bounced. Books tumbled off broken
shelves. Fire licked at the pages. More smoke. More
disorientation. Kruger yelling something she couldn't
hear, and—

The hum in her veins intensified.

Ferguson bared her teeth and, with a low snarl, entered the flow. Deep down, dark and brutal, she
sensed her power gather. Foreign, yet potent. Impatient, yet waiting, unable to rise without her consent.

A monster. A force of nature. The other half of her,
the one she'd never wanted to acknowledge. Always
there, slithering below the surface. Needing, wanting,
willing to help, if only she let it. In the midst of a
firestorm, she turned toward the power, embracing the
new her as the old one burned away. Reborn, she
watched lightning arc between her fingers, flashing
out, raging in, urging her to unleash it.

Her shock faded. New understanding replaced it
as the two halves of her—human and Magickind—
fused, creating a whole.

Instinct her guide, Ferguson threw her hands out,
palms toward the explosion, fingers spread wide, skin
glowing so bright, the brilliance almost blinded her.

She whispered her wishes.

Everything froze mid-whirl. Sucked into the vacuum, deprived of oxygen, the fire died and went out. Splintered wood and shattered glass hung motionless in the air. Ripped from books, paper stopped fluttering as noxious fumes disappeared. Nothing moved but her and Kruger, the sphere rolling, green webbing aglow, coming to rest against scorched bookcases.

"Holy fuck," Kruger rasped, big hands gripping her hips as she settled astride him.

Ferguson ignored him. Gaze on the gaping hole in her bedroom wall, she flicked her fingers. Sparks burst from the tips. Twinkling light wove around and through the debris stuck in suspended animation. Time rewound as she put the explosion in reverse.

Chunks of stone reassembled, then zipped back into place. The wall re-formed around the wide expanse of now-intact window frames. Glass shards met and married in midair, reassembled into lead panes, making broken whole, sealing the room tight as the furniture followed suit, mending in flight before landing back in place.

The last book slipped onto its shelf.

"Fergie—"

"Shields," she snapped, talking to the inn.

A hum powered up as an invisible force field expanded around the hotel.

Kruger flexed his hands, pressing his fingertips into her skin.

She set hers over the back of his, asking for his patience without words.

"Lock it down."

In sync with her, the inn obeyed.

Steel shutters fell like dominoes. Each bang rippled, one after the other, echoing into the night air outside.

Stretching her newfound abilities, Ferguson tilted

her head. The Parkland spoke. She listened, zeroing in, clocking the threat even though she couldn't see it.

Five men. On foot. Running hard, fleeing fast, away from The White Hare and her bedroom.

"Spotlight and track," she said, but the Parkland was already on task, feeding her information, tracking the attackers through the woods. "Leave the hunting to me."

The Parkland protested.

She growled at it, warning it to behave. She needed the assholes alive for questioning, not ripped to shreds by slithering razor-vines and aggressive tree spirits.

"Lass—"

"Gotta move, cowboy." Leaning forward, she planted a quick kiss on the corner of his mouth, then swatted at the sphere. "They're running, but still in the Parkland. If I hurry, I'll catch them."

His lips parted. Awe sparked in his dark eyes. "You found it."

"Total integration," she said, understanding what he meant. "I'm hooked into the hotel and the Parkland."

"You want my help with the arseholes?"

"Yeah. Eyes in the sky."

"Up, lass. Time to hunt."

Smiling at him, Ferguson rocked onto the balls of her feet. The protective web around her dissolved. Green smoke swirled as she stood, grabbed his hand, hauled him to his feet, then murmured, "Clothes, please."

Her closet doors flew open.

Dark fabric whirled across the room. Soft cotton puffed against her skin. One second she stood naked, and the next she was dressed and running for the door. Instinct took her out of her bedroom, down the hall, into the living room. Her feet thumped against hardwood. The French doors opened without her asking. She sped onto the private patio far removed from guests and the public areas. Rubber soles of her running shoes squeaking over flagstone, she jogged down the steps onto the lower level.

Her vision flickered. A switch flipped, allowing her to see in the dark. Gaze narrowed on the edge of the woods, she scanned the ground. Footsteps everywhere, glowing white against black earth, leaving tracks for her to follow.

Looking over her shoulder, she met Kruger's gaze. "You shifting?"

"You got a trail to follow?"

She nodded.

He grinned at her. "Go, lass. I'll track you from the—"

A snarl sounded beside her. Her attention snapped to the right.

The twin statues sitting at the bottom of the stairs moved. Stone teeth became gleaming white fangs. Alarm tightened her chest. She breathed through it, backing away a little at a time as stone transformed into living beings—huge creatures, a pair, one male, one female. Half lion, half dog, a bladed horn jutting from the center of each one's forehead. Massive paws tipped with hooked, lethal-looking claws. Long, shaggy black manes around a lionesque head with short, tufted ears. Sleek body covered in hard scales overlaid with dark gray fur. And...

Bright blue eyes with vertical pupils fixed on her.

"Shit," she muttered, glancing at Kruger from the corner of her eye.

Boots planted on the upper patio, he shifted his

weight, widening his stance. She felt his muscles tense in preparation, sensed his magic spark as the pair prowled toward her.

"Kruger, don't."

"*Fazleima*—"

"Give me a second," she said as he prepared to enter the fray, to put himself between her and danger again.

A noble gesture, one she appreciated, but didn't think she needed. Not right now. The lion-dogs might not look friendly, but intuition reentered the equation, opening the vault of knowledge buried deep inside wider, allowing her to access ancient information.

Moving with care, she reached out her hand, fingers tucked under. The male came to her. Hooked claw clicked over hard stone. Time slowed, holding her prisoner as he butted up against her. A purr rumbled up his throat. She smiled, sinking both hands into his mane, ruffling his fur, scratching behind his ears.

"Fucking hell, lass."

Reacting to his disgruntlement, she laughed, then beckoned to the female. Head low, eyes watchful, the beast prowled toward her, sniffed her knuckles, then pushed through to rub along her flank. With a hum of welcome, Ferguson took time she didn't have to introduce herself, rubbing the sensitive spot between their eyes, enjoying the softness of their fur, marveling at their size and—

A gasp sounded behind her.

She heard the slither of scales before a door slammed shut.

A second later, Hendrix murmured, "Oh, my liege —the Haetae."

"The what?" Kruger growled.

"Guardians of the Parkland, protectors to the innkeeper. We haven't seen them in decades. Not since..."

As he trailed off, information flowed from the inn. She flipped through it like a student with a textbook. Finding the right section, she pulled the reason the Haetae had disappeared from the recesses of her mind. "Since my father died."

"Was assassinated," Hendrix said. "Yes, my liege."

All the more reason to catch the assholes who'd tried to do the same to her. Still, she couldn't resist asking, "Did you know him?"

"I served your sire for almost ninety years."

"We'll talk about him later," she said as the Parkland pulled her strings, drawing her attention back to the matter at hand. Grabbing a handful of the male Haetae's mane, she planted her foot on the second stair tread and swung onto his back. It came naturally, as though she'd been riding one all her life. "Shields are up. The White Hare is secure. Reassure the guests. I'll be back after I catch them."

"Oh course, my liege." A gleam sparked in the gorgon's eyes. The tips of his dreadlocks curled up as though smiling at her. "Happy hunting."

A gust of wind blew across the terrace.

Heat pressed against her skin.

She glanced at Kruger. Her breath caught in the back of her throat. Awe and wonder collided as she got her first look at him. God, he was glorious...and huge, so big his bulk eclipsed the large patio. Dark eyes rimmed by a thin ring of crimson landed on her. Her gaze bounced around, taking him in: emerald-green scales, blood-red accents, enormous paws tipped with multi-bladed claws, clusters of spiraling spikes, some big, others small, snaking along his spine. And a barbed tail that looked wicked.

Pleasure and pride bloomed inside her. "Dragon glory."

"Innkeeper magic," he growled, sounding proud. Opening his wings, he leapt skyward. "Get moving, lass."

She watched him go. Instinct whipped through her. Wildness followed, transforming her into a goddess of the hunt.

Tipping her head back, she shouted into the night. Her battle cry echoed, beating through the woodland. A long staff appeared in her hand, one end a lethal blade shaped like a sickle, the other fashioned into a spiked club. With a tug on the Haetae's ruff, she wheeled him around, urging him into a full run.

They sprinted past huge gates into the Parkland. Ancient trees murmured their welcome. Birds and animals called out a greeting. Magic exploded across the landscape, narrowing her focus.

Movement to her left. Shifting shadows to her right. The scent of damp leaves and rich soil as vines flowed like running water, slithering alongside her.

Waking from decades-long slumber, more Haetae joined the hunt. An army of sleek silhouettes running in the darkness. Paws drumming against compact earth, beating through thick forest as she followed the faint glow of footsteps through the Parkland, running down the ones who'd tried to kill her.

16

Thick fog curled over his horns as rain started to fall. Heavy droplets gathered in the ridges of his scales, then rolled, making emerald green look black against the storm-damp sky.

A nice perk. A wee bit of extra insurance.

Not that Kruger needed it.

Protected by his magic, he flew undetected, tracking Ferguson from the air. He possessed the best of the best, a dragon's-eye view, the entirety of the Parkland laid out in front of him.

Dipping his horned head, he angled his wings and dove toward the dense canopy. The tip of his barbed tail whiplashed. A sharp whistling sound sliced through humid air, boomeranging inside the invisibility spell surrounding him.

He barely noticed, didn't care he flew without a wingmate guarding his six...or that danger sharpened its claws on billowing storm clouds. The sinking feeling nipped at his senses. His sonar pinged, radiating out in circles, searching for the threat. He could feel it rising, a crackling force in the distance that told him he was being watched...

And wasn't alone.

Ignoring the warning, he fine-tuned his radar. His night vision sharpened, allowing him to see everything: the rough bark on each tree trunk, every blade of grass and twig in the underbrush, individual raindrops on leaves splashing up and out as Ferguson sped past, aura burning bright through the gloom.

He wanted to intervene, needed to help her catch those who'd attacked the inn—itched to let his exhale loose, carve into the earth, and stop the bastards in their tracks. The idiots had, after all, nearly blown him to pieces too, but...shite. He couldn't bring himself to ruin her fun, or prevent the new innkeeper from finding her stride.

She was learning, evolving as he watched. Leaning into her magic instead of away, discovering herself one mile at a time. What she'd do when she captured her prey, he didn't know. Probably build a campfire and lecture them. Maybe even offer the arseholes a glass of scotch.

Kruger huffed in amusement. Venomous green smoke puffed from his nostrils as he banked into a wide turn to avoid the high bluff.

Ferguson rode straight through it, taking a narrow path cut through solid rock by centuries of wear and tear, erosion sculpted by the spirit of the Parkland.

Buffeted by strong updrafts, he hovered over the crevice, keeping his eyes on her.

Pride tightened his chest. Goddess, she was glorious. Her bioenergy was at full flare, streaking like a long-tailed comet behind her. Evergreen and crimson touched by gold. A gorgeous expression of her power as she rode wild, jumping over streams, pivoting around boulders, leading a pack of Haetae in the hunt.

Exiting on the other side of the bluff, she rode into

a thicket. The field of tall grass swayed. Thick bramble creaked, rasping against the Haetae's scaled sides. Ferguson didn't let up. Strong in the saddle, she crashed through thick underbrush, then dove into another stretch of woodland, following a trail only she could see. Kruger heard the thundering of paws from five hundred feet up—the scraping and clawing, the bloodcurdling howls as the pack caught the enemy's scent.

His pride for her grew. A female on the hunt. Driven. Determined. Smart and strategic as she tracked the enemy, forcing the rabble to run harder, change tack, and search for a new way out.

Kruger grinned, baring the tips of his fangs. His mate was incredible, a sight to see as she upped the pace, directing the pack from her perch atop one of them, commanding the Haetae like she'd been born to lead them.

A city girl from another country. A magic wielder who met and matched him—a female he'd never be able to hurt with the venom bubbling in his veins. She absorbed his toxicity instead, turning it into something sweet and extraordinary. Such an unexpected gift. One he didn't deserve, but now must decide whether to accept.

Fear sliced through him. He swallowed past the knot making a permanent home in the center of his chest.

Bloody hell, but...he wanted to keep her. Even knowing he should let her go, he yearned to build a life with Ferguson. A terrible idea. Dangerous for him; potentially lethal for her.

Claiming her in the way of his kind was the height of selfishness. His magic burned hotter than other Dragonkind, his volatility dove much deeper. And his bloodline? Fuck, it was as heinous as his sire's history. Making her his would only damage her in the end—diminish her authority as the innkeeper, taint any children they might have together, leaving her alone to raise his infants if the global Dragonkind community discovered who had sired him.

His was a warrior race. None of them would go lightly. His own pack included. Forgiveness would never be part of the equation. The second his kind discovered Silfer's son lived in the earthy realm, the hunt would begin. He'd be forced to run for the rest of his life. And Ferguson...

He drew a choppy breath.

Shite.

His mate was the innkeeper. Her place was here—in the Parkland, providing sanctuary, seeing to the health and care of any Magickind who visited. She couldn't leave. If his secret came out, he couldn't stay, which meant he should fly away now, leave her to the hunt, trust her to deal with The White Hare's enemies in her own way. Do the right thing instead of the selfish one.

Twin beacons raged onto his radar.

He turned into the signal, hunting for—

A flash exploded across the night sky, lighting up his peripheral vision.

Electricity sizzled around him. Raindrops evaporated. Storm clouds stilled. He dodged, losing sight of Ferguson, twisting into a spine-bending flip to avoid the blast. He should've heeded the warning, taken his attention from Ferguson long enough to assess the threat. A stupid mistake. He acknowledged it a second before the invisible wave struck like a supercharged tsunami.

His head whiplashed. Kruger felt his scales crack

and split open. He smelled his own blood as agony detonated like a bomb, making it impossible to breathe.

Choking on bile, he hung in the open air, fighting to stay airborne. Too little, too late. A second surge hit him. Electrical current curled nasty claws around him, cutting through flesh to reach his bones.

His magic flickered like a dying light bulb.

Clinging to consciousness, he clocked the Danes in the distance. Fuck. After months of playing keep-away, the bastards had arrived with firepower so powerful, he couldn't shake the net closing around him, or counteract its effects.

Kruger heard one of the warriors laugh.

The bastard shocked him again.

High voltage. Brutal in intensity. No hope of escape as the violent current picked him up then dragged him down, driving him horns-first into the ground.

17

The glowing footprints grew brighter at the edge of the clearing. Staring through a break in the trees, Ferguson tugged on the Haetae's mane. He obeyed without hesitation, slowing from run to walk, settling into a prowl, keeping his head low as his shoulder blades bobbed. The pads of his paws were silent against the compacted earth on a well-traveled trail that led to an open space beyond the edge of the woods.

The buzz inside her head amplified, feeding her information.

A crossroads, of sorts. With multiple paths leading in different directions. Pathways that intuition told her the men she hunted knew well and visited often. A gathering place, then, but...for whom?

Shifting sideways, she saw five shadows wearing dark gray cloaks, kneeling in the center of the clearing, swords unsheathed and lying on the ground in front of each one.

Dread dripped through her, hitting her like the raindrops pattering against the leaves overhead. A drizzle, nothing that would impede her progress, or mess with her visibility.

Thank God. Nerves and a bad case of *what the hell am I doing?* were already messing with her head. She appreciated the fact Mother Nature didn't feel the need to pile on.

Glancing skyward, she looked for Kruger. He might be up there, flying overhead. He might not. She couldn't tell or see much of anything. The leafy canopy was too dense, the branches too big, the tree-tops so full deep shadows reigned, lording over the forest floor.

Jakamo, the Haetae she rode, snarled. Zensi, his mate, growled in return, setting off a series of low, quiet rumbles from the entire pack. Prickles attacked the nape of Ferguson's neck, then streamed down her spine as the cascading chorus fell like dominos, spinning around the clearing. A warning from the Haetae protecting her...and the Parkland.

Problem was, she didn't speak their language. At least not fluently yet, which left a lot open to interpretation. One thing for sure, though—the Haetae disliked her hesitation. The pack wanted to attack.

Another low snarl rippled from Jakamo. The flash of his fangs in the gloom obliterated all doubt. He disagreed with her approach, finding it too tentative. Ferguson couldn't argue the point. She didn't like how she felt much either, but caution seemed like the smart approach. Even with her newfound abilities, the situation was anything but certain. Charging in without getting the lay of the land first might get him —and her—killed.

Something Kruger would no doubt take personally. And the last thing she needed was a pissed-off dragon warrior roaring around the Parkland. Hendrix would have a coronary. The inn would retaliate, and she'd end up stuck in the middle, playing peacemaker, trying to placate Kruger and his pack...if she made it out alive.

The realization clawed through her, leaving deep gouges.

Her chest tightened. Ferguson breathed through the tension and, turning inward, searched for courage. She wasn't defenseless. She wasn't alone. She wasn't a little girl being bullied in a houseful of assholes. The Haetae were with her. Kruger was on overwatch. The Parkland stood at her back, feeding her magic, upping the intensity until she felt it crackle in her veins.

Her attackers didn't hold the upper hand here. As the innkeeper, she did.

Repeating it like a mantra to herself, she urged Jakamo forward.

A gust of wind blew over the treetops. The sound of chanting in a foreign language wove a path through the trees. Jakamo's muscles quivered in preparation for attack.

Ferguson soothed him with gentle strokes and kept his pace steady. Holding him back was no doubt a bad idea, but curiosity urged her to reconsider. She needed to know who her attackers were and why they'd tried to kill her. More information was better than less. The power to change a life and shift circumstances always came with knowledge. Consider the issue from all the angles, then decide. A lesson her mother taught her. Myriam McGilvery had been thorough, taking pains to ensure Ferguson understood and never rushed to judgment, so...

Time to put lesson number one into practice. No leaping before she looked.

She'd gain more insight by speaking to the men kneeling inside the clearing than from having the

Haetae tear them apart. Understand the who. Deconstruct the why. Formulate a plan to deal her attackers and the fallout.

Kruger would no doubt roll his eyes at her restraint. Killing those she hunted—immediately and without mercy—was the easy thing to do. Taking the time to puzzle it out and determine the extent of the threat was the right one.

Jakamo growled again.

"Easy," she whispered to him. "Let see what's what, yes?"

He chuffed, the sound one of supreme unhappiness.

Her lips twitched. "Relax. We've got them surrounded. They're not going anywhere."

His ears swiveled, flattening against the side of his head.

Ferguson bit down on a laugh. His reaction—and obvious disgruntlement—wasn't funny. Nothing about the situation was *funny*, but she couldn't deny she was enjoying the exchange. The weird conversation with Jakamo settled her, confirming she belonged, as the Haetae accepted her, absorbing her into their pack.

Claws rasping against the forest floor, Jakamo respected her pace and slunk forward. The scent of damp earth and dead leaves rose, flickering across her senses. Perception contracted. Night vision pinpoint sharp, she sent her magic roaming. Information came back, providing details, allowing her see, hear, and smell *everything*: birds nestling in nearby trees, fish swimming in a distant river, the mole burrowing underground beneath Jakamo's paws. The heart of the Parkland beating in her veins.

Something animalistic ghosted through her.

Her hand flexed around the staff she carried. The leather grip rasped against her palm. She twirled it like a baton, reassured by its weight, watching the wicked sickle-shaped blade flash in the low light.

The chanting grew louder.

A soft buzz hummed between her temples.

Directing the Haetae, she walked Jakamo out of the recesses of the wood into the clearing. Deep shadows faded. Fed by the cloud-covered moon, faint light spilled across cloaked figures with hoods up, kneeling in the dell's center, surrounded by strange symbols drawn in the dirt—a series of precise vertical lines intersected by perfect circles.

Recognition flicked its thorny tail. Ancient knowledge flowed unimpeded from an unknown source. Detailed accounts from a bygone era, facts and figures, history she'd never learned, but now knew by heart.

Her eyes narrowed. "Druids."

The chanting stopped.

"Order of the Oak."

Gaze shielded by the edge of his hood, the leader said, "No longer, but we will regain our honor and what has been lost."

Realization struck, and understanding followed. An ancient feud between her family and the order. One set in stone, fueled by hatred and a sense of entitlement.

The men she confronted wanted what the Goddess of All Things had gifted to her father a century ago, what she'd inherited and now enjoyed—a symbiotic relationship with The White Hare and the land it sat upon, the intertwining of life forces and the magical abilities the tight weave produced. The leader and his followers were extremists who'd strayed from their principles and original mission, seeking power instead of harmony with nature.

There would be no reasoning with them. The ideology was rooted deep, obliterating logic, making it impossible for them to listen to what she had to share.

Ferguson drew a deep breath. God help her. She'd hoped it wouldn't come to this, prayed something else was going on, but wishing and hoping never made a thing so. Nothing to do now but end the standoff and do what must be done.

Throwing her foot over Jakamo's neck, Ferguson hopped down. Her feet connected with the ground. Sixteen strong, the Haetae pack stalked in from the outer rim of the clearing, tightening the circle, surrounding men who claimed to be Druids, but no longer were.

"The Parkland will never accept you." Staff in hand, she walked toward the five, stopping before she stepped on the symbols carved into the dirt. A warding spell, one meant to discourage her, to keep her out of striking distance. Not that it would. The men were in the Parkland, a place where she ruled. She wanted to show mercy, but knew she couldn't. Not without endangering the inn, and every member of her staff along with the guests. "It doesn't want you here."

The lead Druid hissed, revealing teeth filed into sharp points.

Jakamo bared his fangs.

She closed her eyes, not wanting to do what needed to be done. Sick to her stomach, she shifted her weight to the balls of her feet, finding her stance naturally, as though she'd trained as a warrior and fought all her life. "God forgive me."

Tipping his head back, the leader shouted, "We are legion!"

"Legion!" the others roared.

Startled birds took flight.

The long staff whirled over her head as her body spun. Magic gathered speed. Bright light flashed as the curved blade sliced down, met flesh, and cut through bone. She heard five heads hit the turf and roll, but didn't look. Instead, she heard the pack of Haetae howl and the Parkland rumble, drinking the enemy's blood as it flowed, soaking into the ground at her feet.

Holes opened beneath the bodies. Tree roots rose like claws and gathered the remains, dragging the dead men deep into the earth.

"Fuck," she muttered, tears in her eyes. One fell. Another followed, tipping over her lashes, running down her cheeks.

The guilt. God, *the guilt*. So much regret that numbness invaded, making legs go weak.

Drawing a shaky breath, Ferguson planted the end of her staff in the ground and leaned on it. Head bowed, throat so tight it hurt to breathe, she offered up a silent prayer for the fallen.

Enemies or not, she hated what she'd just done. *Hated* it. Taking another's life wasn't part of her make-up. She would've preferred to lock the Druids away, give them a life sentence instead of becoming judge, jury, and executioner. Too bad the world she now occupied didn't make those distinctions. Cause and effect. The Druids' attack, their attempt on the innkeeper's life, settled the issue. No negotiating with the Parkland or denying what it demanded—death to the perpetrators by her hand. A clear message sent to any others who might attempt it.

Jakamo butted her with his head.

With a quick swipe of her sleeve, Ferguson wiped the tears away, wishing things were different, wanting a hug so badly she glanced skyward, searching for Kruger in the dark. His arms would feel good wrapped around her right now. His solid presence, reassuring warmth, and straight talk—the brutal honesty he enjoyed shocking her with so much—would settle her in ways she didn't understand, but refused to question.

Stark and unyielding, a yearning for him opened inside her. Air shuddered in her lungs.

The Haetae teamed up, prowling around her, taking turns nudging her with wet noses, pulling at her jacket with sharp teeth.

On a jagged exhale, Ferguson opened her eyes. A death grip on her staff, she pushed to her feet. "Okay, guys. Time to—"

A web of lightning flashed in the distance, shredding the darkness.

A sonic boom shook the ground.

Pain sliced across the nape of her neck as the Parkland shrieked in warning.

With a curse, Ferguson grabbed a fistful of Jakamo's mane. She mounted fast, urging him into a full gallop. Balanced on his back, she sped out of the clearing into the forest. A ping sounded inside her head. A grid flashed on her mental screen, providing a detailed map of the Parkland. Reading the lines, following each blip, she adjusted Jakamo's trajectory. South by southwest, on the edge of her territory. She sensed the fracture and ripple, tapping into Kruger's pain.

He was in deep trouble, with no help in sight.

Urgency slammed through her. Primal instinct drove her forward. She didn't know why or question how she knew. Ferguson listened instead, locking on to the beacon he threw off like pheromones, tracking his location, streaking across the Parkland, terror riding her hard as she felt his heartbeat slow and his life force begin to fade.

18

The putrid smell of burned flesh made his stomach lurch as Kruger dragged himself up the side of a crater. Thirty feet deep, maybe more. A hole he'd made when he slammed headfirst into the ground.

His long claws carved through loose earth. The shattered tips of his horns oozed a mixture of venom and blood—the least of his injuries. The slice along his side was so deep it reached bone. The hole in his belly worried him more. And his back leg? Busted. Useless. Hanging limp, dangling behind him as he clawed up the rise.

Agony blurred his vision.

Still...he reached up, pulled forward, over and over, his goal, the lip of the crater. Each painful claw-and-drag stabbed him in the chest, chipping away at his resolve. He fought through it, air rasping against the back of his sore throat, body shaking, muscles burning, but...

Fuck. He wasn't going to make it.

He felt the fade coming. Heavy blood loss had sapped his strength, making forward progress slow and unsteady.

Stubbornness kept him going. Hope did the rest. Some momentum—no matter how small—was better than none, given who hunted him.

Sheared from his hide by the lightning web, scorched scales flaked off his sides, leaving a trail of iridescent green chips in his wake. Kruger kept his gaze on the top of the rise. He tapped into fury, using rage to help him climb out of the hole. He must get there before the heavy fog cleared. The second he lost ground cover, the Danes would grow brains and get a clue, pinpoint his location from the air, move in for the kill, and finish him off.

His stomach heaved as sticks and stones clawed across open wounds. Goddess, it hurt, hurt so fucking bad, and still he refused to look down. He wouldn't survive seeing the damage. It didn't matter that he felt the gaping hole in his belly...or the blood running down his legs. Seeing was believing, and right now, all he wanted was to believe he had enough strength left to reach the recesses of the forest.

Ferguson was in there...somewhere.

Digging deep, Kruger tapped into bond he shared with her. On the move. Running fast, but...shite. He couldn't tell in which direction. His circuitry was fried. His sonar was damaged, so warped he couldn't tell up from down, never mind get an accurate lock on her.

Kruger sent a signal out anyway in the hopes of finding her. He needed her to stay away, to remain safe instead of doing what he suspected she would— charge in and try to save him. He may have only just met her, but Kruger knew his female well. The instant she realized he was in trouble, she'd come for him. No hesitation. No thought to her own safety. Little care for his wishes. The way Ferguson tackled problems and faced adversity told him she would leave the Parkland to help him.

Good for him, maybe, but too fucking dangerous for her.

The territory she governed fed her magic. The second her feet left its soil, her abilities would flatline, opening her up to an attack. He could feel the Danes looking for him. It wouldn't be long before the pair found him. Which made him work harder to get out of the hole. Not to save himself, but to protect her. No matter how strong, Ferguson was no match for the dragon warriors searching the sky.

Reaching the top, he hauled his bulk across open ground. A rasp of pain left his throat. He gritted his teeth and kept going. Almost there. Just a wee bit farther. Another couple hundred meters, and he'd reached the edge of the Parkland, be safe inside a place that not only recognized him as Ferguson's mate, but accepted him as well.

Blood dripped into his eye. He blinked the haze away and—

Something big slammed into the ground beside him. A tremor rumbled through the dell. Trees swayed. Fog swirled. Kruger bared his fangs, gathering the last of his strength to turn and fight.

Static blew into his head.

"Relax." A huge paw landed in front of his face. *"'Tis only me, laddie."*

"Wallaig," he rasped, trying and failing to push himself upright.

"Donnae move." Orange-red flames flared in his periphery. Heat rolled in on a soothing wave as his friend conjured a cloaking spell, casting a wide net. Good call. Thick fog provided protection, but invisibility

added an extra layer. If luck held, it might buy Wallaig the time he needed to haul Kruger's arse to safety.

"Wallaig—the Danes. Two males. A lightning dragon and a—"

"Clocked 'em, laddie. Came in soft, under radar. They donnae yet know I'm here."

Relief struck like a mailed fist as he breathed through another round of agony. *"Make sure."*

"Already done." The air warped as his XO shifted forms. A second later, human hands touched him, poking at his wounds. *"The arseholes are still searching. Downed you. Didnae pay any attention tae where you crashed. Fucking Danes. Imbeciles, the lot of 'em."*

"Levin? Ran?"

"I'm alone, brother. I sent them on tae Edinburgh. I didnae know you'd been hit, and the others need help."

"Why?"

"Firefight."

"Grizgunn?"

"Aye."

"Fuck," Kruger said, part growl, mostly groan. Injured, in pain and still, he felt his temper rise. The news pissed him off. Goddamn Danes. Just his fucking luck. After months of nothing, then weeks of hoping, wishing, *praying* for a fight, of course Grizgunn had picked tonight of all nights to poke his head out of his hidey-hole. *"I'm missing it."*

Wallaig huffed.

Kruger hissed as his friend prodded a sore spot.

"Shite, Ruger. You're a right mess."

"Need tae... Gotta..."

"Get tae yer female," Wallaig said. *"I know it. Just hold on a—"*

"Go, brother. Leave me here. Join the fight; go help the others."

A beat of silence, then, *"What the fuck?"*

"I'm a lost cause, Wallaig. I'm not going tae make it."

"Bullshite."

"I've lost too much blood."

"Ruger—"

"I need you tae listen tae me now. Listen good, brother. A message from a dying male. Take what I say tae Cyprus and the others. I need them tae know...I..."

His voice cracked as his vision faded, going black around the edges.

Deep in the agony, Kruger struggled to stay awake, to say what he needed to say. He'd been foolish, beyond arrogant—so full of pride, hiding who and what he was, guarding his heart along with his secret. Lying in the dirt, bleeding out, none of it mattered anymore. Not his pride. Not his fear of rejection...or the need to protect his brothers-in-arms from a phantom threat that hadn't yet struck.

Under a black sky, with his enemies close, only one person mattered—Ferguson.

Her safety meant everything. He'd die over and over—again and again—just as long as he knew she'd live her life happy and safe, free of the filth his sire smeared on him.

"Laddie, you're delirious."

"I'm not. I'm not," he said, desperate for the truth to win out. *"I need you tae know—for her. If the worst should happen, if Dragonkind comes looking for me and finds Ferguson, I need tae know my mate will be protected. Despite our bond, she's innocent, Wallaig. I didnae tell her. She doesn't know who I am. About my sire and what he did. You need tae know, so you can protect her. Promise me, mon. Promise that you'll—"*

"I know, Kruger."

"Nay, you donnae. I'm—"

"*Silfer's son,*" Wallaig said, shocking the hell out of him. "*I know all about you, Ruger. I was there when the Goddess of All Things visited Leonid all those years ago. I watched her place you in his arms. Leonid accepted you gladly. In return, the goddess gave him energy-fuse—the sacred words tae the mating ceremony—then told him where tae find Imogen.*"

"His mate?"

"*Aye.*"

"Do the others—"

"*Cyprus knows. When we voted him in as pack commander, I told him. Felt he had the right tae know. And before you worry yerself silly about that too, he doesn't give a shite. Never has, never will. Nor will any of the others.*"

"But—"

"*Shut up and shift, Ruger. I need tae move you, but I willnae get verra far with you like this.*" A sharp tug, and Wallaig rolled him over, exposing his belly wound. "*Jesus.*"

"Told you."

"Where's Ferguson? At the inn?"

"*Nay.*"

"Are you able tae track her? Can you guide me tae her?"

Listening to his friend, Kruger shifted from dragon to human form. The pain intensified. He groaned and curled in on himself. "*Too late. She willnae be able tae—*"

The thunder of paws rattled through the quiet. The ground beneath him trembled.

A shout came next. "Kruger!"

"Fuck," he growled as her voice rolled over him. Pleasure trickled through him. His dragon revived, engaging energy-fuse, connecting with her through the mating bond, needing to feel her. "*Fazleima...*"

"Thank the goddess," Wallaig said.

"Fuck," Kruger muttered again. "Donnae let her, Wallaig. Donnae let her leave the Parkland. The Danes'll spot her. They'll—"

"Too late."

The thump of small feet across thick turf. Skidding. Sliding. Heavy breathing and the chaotic beat of her heart. He sensed it all as she sprinted toward him, but couldn't move. All he could do was wait—hope and pray Wallaig kept his word and Ferguson made it across the dell in one piece.

Big hands pressed into Kruger's shoulder, Wallaig tensed. "Brace, Ruger."

Something cold and smooth slithered around him. "What—"

"Vines," Wallaig said, holding him steady. "They came with her."

Knees landed in the dirt beside him. "God, God, oh my *God*. Kruger...tell me what to do. What do I do?"

Incapable of moving, he lay with his eyes closed. Thick vines curled up and over his body, securing their hold on him. They tugged, dragging him toward the edge of the forest as Ferguson shuffled alongside him and he drank her in. Fuck, but she felt good. Didn't matter that she wasn't touching him. Didn't matter that he was dying. Not anymore. Her proximity, the soothing scent of evergreens and candy canes, was all he needed.

"He's in a bad way, Ferguson. You need tae touch him. Skin tae skin, lass."

"Who're you?"

"Wallaig."

"You coming with, or staying here?"

"I go where he goes."

"Good. Now—"

"*Fazleima*," he said in protest.

"Quiet, cowboy. Now's not the time for back talk."

Wallaig snorted in amusement.

All business, Ferguson ignored Kruger's faint protest, instead doing what he feared most: stripping off her hoodie, pressing close, putting herself in danger to save him. He tried to shake his head. She murmured, then lay down and tucked in, aligning her body with his, palms pressed to his bare skin. The Meridian surged. White-hot current arced through him. Pleasure and pain slashed, blazing a trail through his veins.

Magic detonated.

Her bioenergy whiplashed.

Wallaig cursed.

Kruger bared his teeth as the bond twisted, sucking him into a whirlpool of sensation. He couldn't see. He couldn't hear. All he could do was feel the beauty of his mate and the life-sustaining energy she fed him. Energy-greed bit, killing his control, loosing unimaginable need. Hooked deep, unable to stop, Kruger took everything she gave, feeding fast, drawing too much, making Ferguson jerk as he sank into the abyss and pulled her under.

19

THE INNKEEPER'S COTTAGE — FOUR
HOURS SHY OF THREE DAYS LATER

F ire crackling in the hearth, Ferguson sat cross-legged in an armchair with a leather-bound ledger open in her lap. The smell of smoke and cedar combined, bringing little comfort as she trailed her fingertip over columns of figures. Lots of numbers. More than a few notations in the margins. Some scribbled by Hendrix. Most of it written by her.

She glanced at the stack she'd already flipped through piled on the desk across the room. Such a regal piece of furniture. Massive, rooted by turned legs to the wooden floor. Her father's, well used by him in the ninety years he'd cared for The White Hare.

A pang belled through her until her soul ached. Icabod McCrae—her father. She knew his name now, had even seen his picture. Just the latest tidbit of information delivered by Hendrix.

Every time her major-domo delivered food from the inn to her private cottage, traveling the garden path that reached deep into the woods, he gave her something new. One of her father's journals. Another story about his life, anecdotes of his tenure as innkeeper. Sometimes the gorgon's stories made her laugh. Sometimes they made her want to cry. She drank in each one anyway, like parched earth did rain, needing to understand her history and the radicalized group of Druids who'd stolen her time with the man who'd loved her.

Hendrix tried to be gentle about it. He never gave her more than she could handle, feeding her information at the rate she needed to receive it.

The ledgers, though, were a real boon. She'd been poring over the numbers for days, learning about the inn's financial health, identifying areas of improvement. She used accounting and her business acumen as a distraction, waiting for Kruger to wake up, praying every second of every day that he did.

Three days.

She closed her eyes as worry set off a chain reaction.

Almost three days since the attack.

All the what-ifs came calling, banging around inside her head, making her believe she hadn't reached him in time. The fact he was still breathing did nothing to alleviate her fears. He was unconscious, maybe even in a coma, and she didn't know what to do. Listen to Wallaig and feed Kruger another round of healing energy? Scream and try to shake him awake?

Ferguson frowned as the column of numbers went wavy. She clenched her teeth. No more tears. She refused to allow any more to fall. Curling into Kruger every day and crying was wearing her out. He needed to wake up. She wanted to stop her mind from running down all the what-ifs. What if she'd been quicker? What if she'd gotten to him sooner? What if she lost him before she ever really got a chance to know him?

Drawing a shaky breath, she glanced toward the

bed. Pushed into an alcove jutting out the side of the one-room cottage, Kruger lay unmoving, eyes closed, chest rising and falling at even intervals.

The touch of color in his cheeks gave her hope. Something to cling to in a sea of uncertainty. Yesterday, he'd still been in bad shape, so close to death Wallaig refused to leave, summoning Amantha—his mate—to the cottage instead of flying home with his packmates to the Scottish lair.

Fast asleep, back flat against the leather couch, Wallaig slept like the dead now, Amantha tucked against his side, her head beneath his chin, his arms tight around her.

Ferguson's throat tightened. She wanted what Amantha had—Kruger's arms tight around her, instead of remaining limp at his sides each time she snuggled in for another energy feeding, pacing herself the way Wallaig had taught her.

"Dude," a voice whispered. "Lighten up. He's still breathing, ain't he?"

Ferguson blinked. Her head snapped toward her father's desk.

Perched on the edge, bleach-blond hair sticking straight up, Jethro rolled a joint and raised a brow.

She battled through her need to cry. "Where the hell have you been?"

"The North Sea, bro," her dead friend said. "Radical, dude. Totally extreme. The waves are, like, a hundred feet high."

"Have you seen Cuthbert?"

Jethro rolled his eyes. "Visited the inn. Gotta say, nice digs, dude. But the butler's lost his fucking mind. I got outta there the minute he started complaining about the improper use of tablecloths in the dining room."

She laughed through the sudden sheen of her tears.

Thank God for Jethro. It never failed—he always showed up when she needed him, lightening the mood, putting things into perspective, invading her space with his irreverent attitude...and the pungent scent of weed.

With a flick of his cheap lighter, he lit the end of his joint. He squinted through the smoke, then blew on the end. The tip burned bright orange. The acrid smell increased. Ferguson shook her head, about to tell him to put it out, like she always did, and—

"What the fuck?"

The curse snapped her gaze toward the bed.

Dark brows furrowed, up on one elbow, Kruger wrinkled his nose. "Who the fuck are you?"

Jethro's mouth fell open. "Dragon dude—can you see me?"

Ferguson tossed the ledger aside. The heavy volume landed with a thump on the floor. Chanting, "Thank you, God, thank you, God, thank you, God," she raced across the cottage, heart throbbing, mind burning, her relief so stark it hurt to breathe.

"Fergie."

Kruger's deep baritone curled around her. Her chest heaved. A sob tore from her throat. She ran through the pain, her gaze on him, only one thing on her mind. She needed to touch him, hold him, make sure that she wasn't dreaming, and he was really awake.

20

L ong hair flowing in waves behind her, Ferguson entered the bed at full tilt.

Kruger braced for impact. A wise decision given she didn't slow. Planting her knee on the edge of the mattress, she launched herself at him. He grunted as she slammed into his chest. Rolling with the momentum, ignoring the dead, pot-smoking male perched on the desk, he wrapped his arms around her.

She snuggled in.

Ripping the covers away, he fit her small frame to his much larger one. She whispered his name. He held her tighter, absorbing her shivers, registering her upset, regretting it even as relief hit him hard. Goddess, she was sweet, willing to show the depth of her feelings instead of hiding them away. The bond between mates was powerful. An unstoppable force fueled by primal instinct and intense need, scorching him with the desire to soothe her.

Her breath hitched. She burrowed deeper, trying to get closer.

Kruger adjusted his hold and, brushing her hair aside, palmed the nape of her neck. He pressed his other hand to her lower back, then turned his head, and set his mouth against her temple. Three points of contact against her skin, and energy-fuse sparked. The Meridian unfurled, opening a channel inside him. Her bioenergy flared. He drifted into the stream, loving the feel of her, embracing the gift as his dragon fed her from the source, soothing her the only way he knew how. With profound connection. With intense closeness. With him abandoning the emotional guards that had protected him for years, but no longer served to keep him safe.

He didn't need to be guarded with Ferguson. She nourished him, accepted him, wanted him in ways he felt soul deep, and yet, for some reason, still didn't believe he deserved. His mate was beauty and light. He was death and destruction, a warrior without equal, incapable of compromise.

Self-preservation urged him to reestablish his boundaries. The bond he shared with her refused to allow it, upping the ante by cracking him open, pushing him into places he'd never gone before, but felt right with Ferguson in his arms.

Firming his grip on her, he hooked her knee over his hip. As his thigh settled between hers, Ferguson whispered in welcome, kissed the underside of his jaw, and held on tighter.

"God, Kruger," she said against the base of his throat.

He drew a long breath. "Baby, calm down. It's all right."

"I didn't think you were going to wake up."

"I'm awake, lass," he murmured. "How long was I out?"

"Almost three days."

"Shite."

"Wallaig said... But then I thought... And you weren't... So, I just, you know."

"What?"

"Started praying."

"Bloody hell, lass."

"You scared me."

"I know."

"I want to kick you."

He grinned against her temple. "Normal, under the circumstances."

"It isn't funny. You almost died."

"I didnae. I'm hale and whole, Fergie, mostly thanks tae you, but...next time"—he paused for effect —"if there ever is a next time, I'll tan yer hide if you donnae leave well enough alone."

Her muscles tensed. She stilled against him. "Excuse me?"

"You heard me," he said. "You donnae put yerself in danger for any reason, Ferguson. Not for me or anyone else. I'm a dragon warrior, born and bred. I understand war. I know the stakes. Silfer's blood runs through my veins. I protect you. You donnae do the same for me."

"That's crap. I mean, seriously...total effing crap."

"*Fazleima*—"

"It is, Kruger." With a wiggle, she pulled away from him. Getting the message, he loosened his hold on her. He read the intensity in her expression before he heard it in her voice. "You wanted me to feel the bond between us—well...I *feel* it. It's deep in my bones, in the beat of my heart, in the threads connecting my soul to yours. You can't undo it. Neither can I, which means if you're hurt—if you need me—I'm not going to sit at home eating bonbons or—"

"Bonbons?" the dead guy said, grinning like a madman.

Kruger glared at him over the top of her head.

The arsehole shrugged, then blew out a stream of smoke.

"—drink a cup of effing tea." Green eyes dark with temper, Ferguson scowled. "You think you get to dictate the terms of energy-fuse. You don't, I don't, so suck it up, cowboy, and deal. I'm the effing innkeeper. I can take care of you, me and the rest of your dragon horde, without breaking a sweat."

"Dude, chill. I think he gets it."

"Shut up, Jethro," she said without looking at him.

"Just saying, bro."

"Seriously? Hello...private conversation," she snapped at the dead guy. Jethro sighed and took another puff. Ferguson turned her attention back to Kruger. "Now...are you getting me?"

"Aye."

"Are you on board or not?"

Fighting a smile, Kruger cupped her cheek. "Do I have a choice not tae be?"

"No."

Kruger laughed. His mate was gorgeous always, but angry, she lit up the room, aura flaming, bioenergy snapping—a sight to behold as she fought for what she wanted, making him realize she wouldn't tolerate half measures. Something he'd been guilty of giving for a very long time. With himself. With his brothers-in-arms. He'd guarded his heart so closely, he hadn't been able to open it to anyone...until now. Until her.

"Baby," he murmured, "we've got things tae talk about."

"Your secret?"

"Among other things."

He had a lot to say—about her attackers, battle strategy going forward, and future living arrangements. Instinct warned him away from discussing his sire. His reluctance was guided by habit, a bad one, something he needed to break. Ferguson was his mate. Trusting her with all of him, every little piece, came with the territory. She deserved his best. His all. Being her male meant he must give her the whole truth, and nothing less.

"But first, can you get rid of the dead guy?" he asked.

"Unlikely." She made a face, one he found adorable. "Jethro does what he wants, when he wants. Can you really see him?"

"Aye."

"Right on, dude. Stands to reason, though."

Ferguson's brows popped toward her forehead. She glanced over her shoulder at Jethro. "How do you figure?"

"Wavelengths, bro. Bandwidth. His matches yours. Perfect pitch," Jethro said, flipping his hands out in an "duh" gesture. "You see me, so now he does too."

"Hate to agree with him, cowboy. It doesn't happen often, but"—tilting her head, she pursed her lips—"he's making sense."

Jethro scoffed at the insult.

Kruger kissed the tip of her nose. "How long have you seen ghosts?"

"All my life."

"Is Jethro the only one?"

She shook her head. "There've been others. Cuthbert's stayed around the longest, though. Oh, and Luther too."

"Luther?"

"His dearly departed cat."

"Fucking hell," Kruger grumbled, envisioning a lifetime full of dead people popping in to visit his mate...and annoying the hell out of him. "Is there any place you're safe from them?"

"Haven't found one yet."

He sighed.

"You're good and stuck now, cowboy."

"Is that where you want me? Truly, Fergie—do you really want tae be stuck with me?" he asked, giving her an out as doubt circled, messing with his head. "Think on it, lass. Do it hard and fast...be honest with yerself and me. I'm not normal by Dragonkind's standards... or any of yers either."

"Normal is overrated. I've never been normal, Kruger," she said, gaze drilling into his. "Do you want me any less knowing I see ghosts, or that I'm the newly appointed innkeeper to The White Hare?"

"I donnae give a fuck who you are, or where you come from," he growled, pissed off by the implication. "You're mine. That's all that matters tae me."

"Then why can't I feel the same way about you?"

His brows collided. "I hadn't thought of it that way."

"Well, start," she said. "I know we're new, and it'll take some time, but one thing I'm sure about—I'm for you, and you're for me. We fit. We're meant to be to-gether. You trust in that, and I will too."

"Fuck, baby.

"Yeah."

"Gone for you, Fergie. In so deep, I'm tangled up in you now." Wrapping a tendril of hair around his fin-gers, he tugged. Her chin tipped up. He kissed her softly, sweetly, with so much feeling she trembled in his arms, feeling the same thing he did. "Having you, feeling the beauty of you...I donnae want tae live without you now."

Tears pooled in her eyes. "You'll never have to, handsome. I've been searching for you my whole life. Looking, hoping, praying...dreaming of the promise of you. I'm not going anywhere."

His chest tightened. "Time and patience, baby."

"Yeah," she whispered. "Little by little, we'll find our way."

"We will, lass. On that, you have my word."

"Outstanding. Finally, someone's talking sense," Jethro muttered, eavesdropping without concern, knowing how much Kruger wanted to, he couldn't kill him. The bastard was already dead. "Time to party! Where's the gorgon? We need booze."

Board shorts flapping, body glowing with ethereal light, Jethro hopped off the desk. His bare feet slammed into the floor. A tremor rocked the cottage. Dust floated down from the timber beam rafters. Furniture shivered. Half-burned logs shifted in the fireplace. The snap 'n pop echoed as the chandelier above the bed swayed.

"What the hell?" Wallaig growled.

Her forehead pressed to the side of his jaw, Ferguson chuckled.

Feeling her happiness in his gut, Kruger grinned. He wanted to be alone with her. Now. But with Jethro rummaging through a cabinet looking for liquor and his packmate half-asleep across the room, making love to Ferguson would have to wait. He'd get his chance to strip her down and love her hard...later.

For now, he would enjoy having her in his arms, rest easy in the knowledge she was happy and safe, forever his—today, tomorrow, for the rest of his nights, and the remainder of his days. She'd helped him find his way. Kruger accepted the truth now. He was his own male— one of honor who'd chosen his own path and wasn't anything like his sire. He wasn't perfect. Mistakes would be made. But no matter how many pitfalls life placed in his path, he'd face each one with Ferguson at his side.

Peace came with the realization. The under- standing he'd finally done something right—and had nothing left to prove—followed, making him hug her tighter. By design or chance, the universe had given him what he needed all along—the innkeeper. A war- rior queen who met and matched him in all ways.

He hadn't lied, after all.

Ferguson was precious. The breath in his lungs. The magic in his veins. The North Star in his stormy sky. Calling him home. Steady in the face of his feroc- ity, possessing the fortitude to take him as he came, unafraid to love him as fiercely as he did her.

A gift.

His mate.

His bright and shining star.

21

B uried under a mound of paperwork, Ferguson sifted through the most recent pile on her desk. Another gorgeous piece inherited from her father, planted in the innkeeper's private office connected by a corridor to the main lobby of the hotel. What she could see of the walnut top polished to a high shine, making her feel needed and important, like she'd been born to sit behind it.

The swivel chair she sat in failed to convey the same message.

The thing was a relic. Seat stuffed with horsehair. Wooden joints loose and wobbly. Old springs in need of a good oiling. She should probably order a new one. Something ergonomic. Sentimentality banished the idea. Her father had sat in the same spot she did now, so...

The quiet creak every time she moved wasn't so bad. No need to complain or look for a replacement. A little TLC, and her father's chair would be as good as new.

Shuffling through a stack of files, she listened to the low hum of chatter drifting through the open door. Some guests checking in, others checking out.

The majority, however, traversed the lobby, heading to the dining room for what Hendrix called the Third Meal.

She glanced at the Grandfather clock ticking in the corner. 4:32 a.m. Nothing unusual about the time.

Magickind kept odd hours. Much different from their human counterparts. Most of her guests woke after lunch and went to bed at dawn. A convenient shift in lifestyle for her. She'd always been a night owl, wide awake into the wee hours, sleeping in late, driving her stepfather insane with her odd sleep schedule.

Now she knew why.

Different biorhythms drove her internal clock, ensuring she stayed alert when magical creatures roamed. A blessing given the aggressive species with powerful personalities and volatile natures who checked into The White Hare.

Finding the correct file, Ferguson yanked the yellow one out of the middle of the stack. Red, purple, and pink folders slid off the top. She flicked the tip of her index finger. The cardstock avalanche stopped mid-tumble without her touching it, then did as she wished and settled back on top of the now straight pile.

Magic.

Her mouth curved.

Incredibly convenient.

Flipping the file open, she skimmed through the list of reservations, memorizing names, dates and arrival times before turning the page. A lot more traffic this week. More and more guests coming and going. Hendrix was in fits of glee. Ascot remained a worry-wart, proselytizing doom, terrified of the ogres who'd checked in yesterday evening.

Unwilling to commit to her major-domo's delight or the Chinchilla's gloomy outlook, Ferguson sat somewhere in the middle. Cautiously optimistic, but ready for anything.

The uptick in traffic, though, gave her hope.

If the occupancy rate held steady for the next month, The White Hare's financial situation would turn around, moving the totals in her ledgers from red into the black. She'd checked the amounts and accounts multiple times. Had asked Kruger to look over the numbers—two pairs of eyes were always better than one—and came to the same conclusion every time.

The inn was not only awake, but thriving. Moving into healthy territory fast, attracting Magickind in the area, and from all over the world, to the Parkland.

The last name on her list proved it.

Henry Biscayne from Savannah, Georgia. An American, like her, but also...

Her eyes narrowed on his pedigree (information required of all guests with an eye to keeping the peace between different magical species staying at the inn). In the last column, Henry had written — Vampire Prince of the Dark Fae.

"Huh," she murmured.

The Dark Fae coupled with vampirism. An odd combination, one that didn't appear anywhere in the Udo's Manual of Mystical Creatures. Not in any of the five volumes. And she should know.

She'd read every single installment, cover-to-cover, in the last two weeks. Necessary time spent. A prerequisite of her job as she memorized origin and breed, learning the likes and dislikes of her guests, breaking down their supernatural abilities to understand each subset. Kruger helped her, pointing out the more dangerous aspects of the individuals who frequented the inn.

Tapping her fingernail against the spreadsheet, Ferguson frowned. Henry Biscayne, Vampire Prince of the Dark Fae. She'd never met him, hadn't seen him when he checked in, but the way he categorized himself bothered her. She pursed her lips. No clue why, but he seemed like someone she needed to watch, just in case things went south and—

A roar shook the lobby, spilling into her office.

Answering snarl followed. Something big collided with something else. A tremor rumbled beneath her feet. Her desk trembled. Multiple picture frames jumped off the wall, nose-dived, then slammed into the wooden floor.

Another roar. More snarling. A high-pitched screech from what sounded like a fairy.

"Crap," she muttered, shoving out of her chair.

Antique glass wheels hissed across the area rug.

Moving from walk to fast jog, she rounded the end of the desk.

Ascot shrieked from the lobby, "My liege, my liege... my liege!"

Ferguson sighed. Something she'd learned about Ascot. He always yelled things in threes. A habit to break him of, but as another roar echoed, she put the problem of the Chinchilla's sensitive nature aside. Conjuring her staff, she strode out of her office, down the short hallway, past the long, gleaming length of check-in desk, into an enormous space capped by a coffered forty-five-foot high ceiling.

Her mind took a quick snapshot.

Two ogres, spiked clubs raised, blackened teeth bared, locked in mortal combat in the middle of the lobby.

One swung a huge club at the other.

Wind gusted through the lobby as the other dodged.

Guests scattered, running for cover.

"Stop," she said with quiet authority. Her hushed tone speared through the lobby. Spinning the bladed end of her staff upright, she strode toward the combatants. "Right now."

Almost twelve feet tall, the offenders paused midfight. Bald heads swung in her direction. Flat noses with slitted nostrils flared. Round eyes blinking, the matched-set-of-ugly assessed her, deciding whether to obey.

She added some incentive. "If you don't, I'll send you to sleep in the stables...with Koerich."

Both ogres blanched.

Ferguson didn't blame them. Bringing the stablemaster into the matter upped the stakes. Koerich was violent and unfeeling. The perfect incentive, an excellent deterrent to anyone, ogres included. No one who wanted to stay in one piece tangled with the Centaur. He was never in a good mood, enjoyed cracking heads open, was so bad-tempered, Ferguson adored him from the moment she met him. Hard not to when faced with a grumpy half-man, half-horse who didn't give a shit who she was, or blink at the power she wielded.

He ruled the stables. The innkeeper could go hang if she didn't like it. End of story, don't bother him with it, as far as Koerich was concerned.

"Now, thankfully, you didn't damage my inn with your foolishness," she said, pausing for dramatic effect. "So, I'm reconsidering my need to kill you."

Alarm in his colorless eyes, ogre number one swallowed.

His partner in crime took a step back, away from her.

She wanted to laugh. Stifling the urge, Ferguson kept her expression stern, scaring the hell out of them as her eyes glowed, shimmering across their pale skin. The pair bowed their heads in shame. She tapped into her connection with the inn. A map of the grounds appeared on her mental screen, providing a list of all ongoing activities.

"There is a combat circle available in the East Garden," she said calmly. "I suggest you resolve your differences there."

Shoulders slumped, the ogres grumbled an apology. Dragging their clubs, the pair trudged toward the exit on the east side of the lobby.

Hiding behind the concierge desk, Ascot popped his head up. Whiskers twitching, a panicked look on his furry face, his ears swiveled back and forth.

A prickle ghosted across the nape.

Strong arms closed around her from behind, enveloping her in warmth. She leaned into the embrace, absorbing his heat, enjoying his scent, loving the way he liked to sneak up on her. Never failed. One moment Kruger was nowhere to be found, the next pressed against her back, holding her tight.

Kissing the shell of her ear, he murmured, "You handled that well, *fazleima*."

"It's not as difficult as it looks."

"For you, maybe. Anyone else—cracked skulls and screams of pain."

Listening to guests come out of hiding and go on their way, she turned in his arms. As her eyes met his dark ones, she smiled. "You're early."

"No joy tonight, lass."

"Nothing at all?"

A muscle twitched along his jaw. "Grizgunn's still hiding. Talked tae some druids in the Cairngorms, but the bastards who planned the attack on you belong tae a splinter group. Radicalized by their leader. Part of a cult now. The Order of the Oak renounced them decades ago."

"You believe them?"

"Didnae say I wasn't going tae keep a close watch on the bastards, Fergie. Levin's all over it. On a fucking rampage."

Finally, some good news.

An ice dragon with a chilly disposition and murder in his ice-blue eyes, Levin took viciousness to new levels. Anyone with half a brain would take one look, turn tail, then avoid him at all costs. Having him involved boosted her confidence. All right, so the lack of progress so far was frustrating, but beggars couldn't be choosy. She'd take what she could get. And honestly? Standing in the circle of Kruger's arms, the getting was pretty damn good.

"What happened at the meeting?" she asked, moving him off a topic that angered him to one that most concerned her.

He shrugged off her question.

Ferguson held firm, refusing to let him off the hook. She understood his reluctance. Really, she did. He was still sensitive about it. Old habits died hard, but allowing him to brush the issue aside wouldn't work. Ignoring open wounds, burying the hurt, never did. Despite his resistance, Kruger needed to talk about it...often. Until he cleared the air and became more comfortable with the truth.

"How'd the guys take the news?"

He sighed.

She waited, her gaze steady on him, wielding silence like a weapon.

"You're not going tae let this go, are you, lass?"

"No."

"Fuck."

"Start talking."

A pregnant pause. Thin slices of time piled on top of one another.

He remained stubborn a moment, then gave in and grumbled, "Wallaig was right."

"Yeah?"

Giving her a squeeze, Kruger dipped his head. His mouth brushed over her cheekbone, ghosted to the edge of her eyebrow, then turned to nuzzle her temple. "None of them give a shite, Fergie. All of them gave me shite, though...especially Cyprus...for thinking my brothers would care who sired me, or where I came from. Vyroth and Tydrin used their fucking fists. Rannock and Levin put me on my arse. I'm never going tae live it down."

"No doubt for the best."

His lashes brushed her skin as he blinked. "What?"

"You need reminding."

"Lass—"

"You do, Kruger," she said, giving him the words he needed to not only hear, but take to heart. "You are not your sire, handsome...you never were. But the fact you've carried that belief around your whole life, burying it deep, letting it fester, keeping your packmates...guys who love you, warriors who would kill to protect you...in the dark speaks volumes. So, yeah. You're going to need reminding every once in a while to keep you from sliding back into old patterns."

"Got you for that."

"Yes, you do." Fisting her hands in the back of his jacket, she tucked her head beneath his chin. "But a little extra insurance never hurt anyone."

"*Fazleima*," he murmured, tightening his grip on her. A burst of chaotic emotion spiked inside him. She quivered in response. Big hand cupping her nape, he pressed his face into the side of her neck. "Marry me."

His words jolted through her.

Air stalled in her lungs. "What?"

"I love you, Ferguson. Marry me. Allow me tae claim you in the way of my kind."

"In a sacred Dragonkind ceremony?"

"Aye."

"You'll give me your mating mark?"

"And I'll wear yers."

Wonder collided with shock, stealing her oxygen. "Holy crap."

He grinned.

"Kruger." Deep yearning opened like a chasm inside her. Instead of turning away like she always did, Ferguson forced herself to look into the abyss. Love and acceptance gazed back. Everything she'd ever wanted. Everything she needed right here, pressed tight against her, holding her in his arms. All she had to do was reach out, grab hold and...

God.

She loved him. Wanted to be his so badly. Wanted it all—to stand inside the ancient circle with him, to listen as he said his vows, to repeat hers back to him. More than anything, though, she longed for his mating mark, to see his tattooed across the backs of her knuckles and hers drawn across his.

Tears pooled in her eyes.

"Can I take that as an aye?"

"Yes." Her breath hitched as she bucked in his

arms. "I love you. I want you, the ceremony, your mark...every little piece of you."

"Every little piece, Fergie. You want it, you got it."

A sob caught at the back of her throat.

Kruger held her through it, tucking her closer, letting her cry, uncaring he stood in the middle of a hotel lobby with werelions, water nymphs, Cuthbert and Hendrix looking on.

Epilogue

The end of Marlborough Street — Edinburgh, Scotland, 4:32 a.m.

STANDING on the back terrace under a ripped black-and-white awning, Callas ignored the pain and planted his palm on the tabletop. His elbow protested the pressure, reminding him of the firefight between the Danes and the Scottish pack. Unbelievably brutal, and enlivening as hell, even though he'd been hit in the crossfire.

Embracing the pain of his still-healing wounds, he leaned in and put more pressure on the joint, punishing himself for his stupidity. Frayed nerve endings squawked. He ignored the strain and reached out, changing the angle of the computer screen.

As he tilted it back, a harmless-looking website loaded—a private forum for serious online gamers. The perfect entry point, a back door into the dark web, one many Dragonkind packs used to relay important information.

A necessary evil, but he hated it anyway, disliking the social aspect along with the idea of using a human invention. His kind weren't meant to communicate with machines. Mind-speak was better, encouraging more meaningful connection. Fewer chances for misunderstanding...or reading a male wrong.

He reread his message, frowned, made a few corrections, added another line of text, then nodded and hit the enter key.

Message sent.

Now came the waiting.

Struggling to be patient, he drew a deep breath. The smell of salt water came to him. He closed his eyes, listening to waves roll onto shore at the end of the street. The ebb and flow drained his tension. He'd already been in tonight, shifting into dragon form to swim the English Channel. His dragon urged him to go back. Walking the half a block to the shoreline and diving in would be easy. Getting past his brothers-in-arms, not so much.

Beauregard and Rune didn't approve of his midnight swims. Neither wanted him out alone, given the dangerous turn their mission had taken, but...a water dragon needed to swim. And he preferred open water to salt baths and swimming pools.

Rechecking his work, he clicked through a couple more forums. Nothing yet. No answer from the pack he needed to meet next. Months of searching had brought him to Scotland. He'd been all over Europe, spending most of his time in Prague, hobnobbing with Dragonkind elite, searching for answers, hunting his quarry, trying get the lay of the land. So far, he hadn't come up with much more than the firm understanding the Archguard—the five dynastic families that ruled Dragonkind—were assholes. Greedy, selfish pricks out for themselves, uncaring of anyone else.

Not that it mattered. His mission didn't include

making friends with the aristocracy. He needed to find one male, and one only.

Done scrolling, he snapped the laptop shut. Bare feet whispering over the cracked pavers, Callas limped down the crumbling stone steps.

Silver gaze flickering in the low light, Rune looked up from his book. The frayed camping chair he sat in creaked, threatening to dump him on the ground. Unconcerned, he raised a dark brow. "All set?"

"We'll see." His gaze roamed the setup in the backyard. A snowdrift took up half of the space, covering up an ocean of green grass. Beauregard was sitting in the middle of it, his ass planted in a chair sculpted out of ice, bottles of Windswept Ale sticking out of the snowbank beside him. Callas raised a brow. "Comfortable?"

"Could be better," Beauregard said before taking a long pull from his bottle.

Callas snorted. "The females just went home."

A gleam sparked in his friend's ice-blue eyes. "Could use a couple more to tide me over till tonight."

Stepping over the lip of the outdoor tub, Callas sank into salt water. A sigh of relief escaped him.

"You should've spent more time with the blonde, Cal," Rune said. "You're not healing right."

"Empty feedings. Insufficient bioenergy for my needs." Leaning his head back against the steel rim, Callas gazed up at the night sky. Wispy clouds. Lots of stars. Pretty place, Scotland. "Fucking unsatisfying."

"You're chasing a dream, brother."

Maybe.

Rune might be right, but Callas didn't care. He needed to know the truth. And whether the intel he'd already gathered pointed in the right direction. Years in prison—locked away for crimes he hadn't committed—had taught him not to fuck around. His deal with the Dragon God and subsequent release into the world had provided the chance he needed to right a wrong, to make amends, and maybe, if he got lucky, build a relationship with the male he'd sired but never met.

Thirty-five years was a long time.

He clenched his teeth. *Was* his son still alive? Had he died without Callas there to protect him? Silfer kept assuring him the infant had survived, but refused to give him any more details. Callas didn't even have a name. No place or date of birth. Nothing but a fucked-up deal with the cruel deity currently pulling his strings.

"Silfer's an asshole," Beauregard said, echoing Callas's thoughts and Rune's sentiment. "He wants what he wants. You give it to him, he'll fuck you over, Cal, and not think twice about it."

No doubt true, but...hope sprang eternal.

He shrugged, brushing aside his wingmate's concern. "He wants his son as much as I want mine."

"Poor bastard," Beauregard muttered. "He won't want Silfer to find him."

"I don't give a shit. The male's a means to an end, nothing more."

After folding the corner of a page over, Rune tossed his novel onto a rusty table. "You don't think he's with the Danes?"

"Didn't get that feeling." Closing his eyes, Callas relaxed deeper into the water. "Time to look at the Scottish pack."

"Suicide," Rune grumbled.

"Probably," Callas said, but nothing ventured, nothing gained.

Such was life. A male took his chances with the

hand he'd been dealt. Good cards? Bad shuffle in a rigged deck? One way or the other, it didn't matter in the end.

THE DRAGON'S HORN — Old Town, Aberdeen

HIS PHONE RANG.

Boots thumping through the quiet of the empty tavern, Levin rounded the end of the bar. Gaze on the bottles sitting on glass shelves lining the mirrored wall, he did a mental inventory. The assorted vodka bottles were topped up. Gin levels were acceptable. Jägermeister untouched, per usual. More Dragon's Breath, the brand of scotch he and his brothers-in-arms owned, needed to be brought out and shelved.

His phone chirped again. With a yank, he pulled the stupid thing out the back pocket of his Levi's.

The notification flashed on screen.

A muscle twitched along his jaw. A new message from some online gaming site, email address attached. His eyes narrowed as his temper flared. Bloody hell, whoever sent it was tenacious, the kind of persistent Levin didn't like unless it came from him.

Gaze glued to the screen, he tapped here and there, engaging his firewall, setting up a covert search to track the bastard. Such a waste of time, but as much as he hated to admit it, he'd let it go on too long. He needed to stop ignoring the arsehole and investigate. Instinct warned him the hacker wasn't human. The language he used in the message gave him away. Which meant Levin must figure out what the male wanted and dissuade him of the notion.

Violently, if necessary.

He hoped the bastard went that way. Toying with the male clogging up his inbox would be satisfying, a well-timed diversion after the clusterfuck with the Danish pack over Edinburgh. Grizgunn, along with the warriors he commanded, had gotten away, gone underground and stayed there until dawn hit the horizon, forcing Levin and his packmates out of the sky. An opportunity lost. A rage-inducing, pansy-ass ploy. The Danes were skilled at hiding, great at turning tail and running, not so hot at fighting to the finish. So aye, he might as well indulge in a distraction. He deserved a bit of fun for his troubles.

Cracking his knuckles, Levin stared at the gleaming bar top. A plan began to form. Nothing complicated, pretty basic stuff in the covert world in which he operated. The email junkie had earned a lesson. A brutal one. Something he planned to deliver before flying in to deal the deathblow.

An ice dragon's dream. Nothing but fun, fun, fun.

Cyprus would no doubt frown on the festivities, reprimand him for his methods, but...whatever. His commander would come around and lighten up in the end.

Shoving his phone back into his pocket, Levin grabbed a wet rag and got back to work, getting ready to open the tavern, looking forward to the night he sank his claws deep, ripped the bastard's lungs from his chest and listened to him squeal.

A NOTE FROM THE AUTHOR

Thank you for taking the time to read Fury of Frustration. If you enjoyed it, please help others find my books so they can enjoy them too.

Recommend it: Please help other readers find this book by recommending it to friends, readers' groups, and discussion boards.

Review it: Let other readers know what you liked or didn't like about Fury of Frustration.

Follow me on Facebook, Instagram and Bookbub to get all the latest news.

Sign up for my Newsletter and get exclusive VIP giveaways, freebies and sales throughout the year.

Book updates can be found at www. CoreeneCallahan.com

Thanks again for taking the time to read my books! You make it all possible.

ALSO BY COREENE CALLAHAN

Dragonfury Scotland
Fury of a Highland Dragon
Fury of Shadows
Fury of Denial
Fury of Persuasion
Fury of Isolation

Dragonfury Bad Boy Shifter Series
Fury of Fate
Fury of Conviction

Dragonfury Series
Fury of Fire
Fury of Ice
Fury of Seduction
Fury of Desire
Fury of Obsession
Fury of Surrender
Fury of Destruction

Circle of Seven Series
Knight Awakened
Knight Avenged

Warriors of the Realm Series
Warrior's Revenge

ABOUT THE AUTHOR

Coreene Callahan is the bestselling author of the Dragonfury novels and Circle of Seven series, in which she combines her love of romance and adventure with her passion for history. After graduating with honors in psychology and taking a detour to work in interior design, Coreene returned to her first love: writing. Her debut novel, *Fury of Fire*, was a finalist in the New Jersey Romance Writers Golden Leaf Contest in two categories: Best First Book and Best Paranormal. She lives in Canada with her family, a spirited Anatolian Shepherd, and her wild imaginary world.